GOING
NOWHERE

LENA NORTH

FAB BOOKS

PRINT EDITION
ISBN: 978-91-88367-35-8

Discover other titles by Lena North:

Birds of a Feather series:
Wilder
Sweet Water
Picture This
Black Snow
Reaper

The Islands:
Seaborn

The Dreughan series:
Courage
Reason
Joy

With gratitude to my parents for providing my genetic makeup, and everything else.

CONTENTS

CHAPTER 1

And so it begins

"What in the everloving fudge did you do?"

"Nothing," I said, wishing I didn't sound so guilty suddenly.

"You got fired from the cushiest dog-walker job in the whole state. You clearly did something."

"I did not," I said, switching quickly from guilty to defiant.

And yeah, that was pretty much a lie but seriously? The dog had totally started it.

"Is Pookie still alive?" Elsa asked, eyeing me suspiciously.

Elsa.

The sweetest girl with the biggest heart in the whole world.

My best friend.

And a unicorn.

At least when she wants to be one, which isn't very often. Elsa works in a library and having a big, white unicorn stomping around would make her boss give her a death-glare over her glasses. Or shush. Since no one glares and shushes like a librarian, most of the time she's just a regular homo sapiens like me.

Except, of course - I'm a witch.

Don't get me wrong, I'm in no way the gnarly, grey-haired and wart filled kind of witch. They live over in Hanksville. I am a white witch from the covenant of Nim, which means that I have no warts at all.

I have black hair, a tall and willowy body, translucent, white skin, and dark brown eyes.

Or, yeah. No.

But I should have.

The thing is; my witchiness comes from my mom but my dad is a huge, white-haired werewolf of Scandinavian descent, and his genes were pretty dominant in the whole creation of me, probably because he's a pretty dominant kind of guy. And since I'm partly a wolf, I got brownish, wavy hair, green eyes, and skin that tan quickly in the summer. There's a faint band of freckles across my nose, and no one in their right mind would call someone with my booty willowy, although that could have less to do with my wolf part and more with the fact that I deal with all the shit life keeps throwing at me by gobbling down unfortunate quantities of anything

Reeces. And cookie dough.

"Of course the stupid thing is alive," I snapped.

"How in the hell could you get sacked, Kitty? You're a dog yourself."

That last bit came from Joel, my other best friend.

Joel is a widget, which is the coolest thing because they are super rare but super useful. And popular, which isn't much of a surprise since widgets communicate with anything controlled by computer code, and changes that code as they wish unless it's protected by another, stronger, widget.

"Am not," I snapped

"Half dog."

I opened my mouth to protest, but we'd had that particular argument since the three of us met en route to detention, outside the principal's office in Saint Honoria of the Immaculate Transformation High School, so I shut it again and glared at him.

He glared back.

When this had gone on for a while, I gave in.

"I just growled, okay?"

I'm not a shifter like daddy, and the three spawns of Satan also known as my brothers, but I have enough wolf in my blood to heal quickly, run fast - and growl in a way that scares the bejeesus out of virtually anyone.

The only animals in our part of the world that don't leave an embarrassing puddle behind when the wolves growl are bears, so of course my darling daddy had to go and get re-married to one. I love my stepmom Janie to pieces, but it would have been a lot easier to get away with shit if he'd picked, say, a fox-shifter or even one of the cats.

"So," Elsa murmured. "You now have no job, no money, no way to pay rent, and as a consequence absolutely no other choice but to move back home."

Crap.

That was an uncomfortably clear, and accurate, summary of my situation.

Double-crap.

I'd have to move back home.

I grew up with my dad, stepmom, and brothers in an enormous house on the outskirts of a small town called Nowhere, and yes, I've heard every stupid joke there is about that name.

Yes, even <insert lame joke here>.

And <insert another annoyingly lame joke here>.

My parents split up two hours and fourteen minutes after I was born, and I rarely see my mom, so no one in town hesitates to call her, "the witch that starts with a b," in my presence. I actually find that hilarious, considering my dad's furry persona, but it's also not wrong.

Two days after leaving dad, and me, Mom got married to a wizard with the fantastically unspellable name Aïdan Azdjakzian. Aïdan is a snooty, highbrow, wave your wand in the face of anyone kind of man that I do not like. My friends and I refer to him as "the Az," and needless to say, he does not like me right back.

Mom and the Az decided to procreate with an embarrassing speed and provided me with four half-sisters. They're also witches, which quite possibly indicates that the genetic makeup of his Aziness isn't as superior as he likes to think.

As is the custom among the witches of Nim, my sisters have names from mother nature, and they're called Rose, Poppy, Lily, and Iris.

I, on the other hand, am called Hibiscus.

Giving me that ridiculous name was probably the bitchiest thing mom has ever done when she so easily could have called me something like Hazel, which is a really whitchy name. It's also my grandmother's name so it would have been completely fitting, but Grandma Hazel has a well-developed and highly sophisticated sense of humor, which means I love her, but Mom doesn't.

So yeah, my mother is Fuchsia de Chamontelette-Azdjakzian, and I am Hibiscus Brown.

My dad is called Biff. Biff Brown. No joke. And he populated the world even quicker than Mom because my brothers are triplets. This is uncommon among the wolves, and unheard of with the bear shifters, which makes it a source of great pride with Dad, who talks way too often about the speed and agility of his swimmers. Since I really don't want to think about semen and my father at the same time, or even in the same millennium, I have learned to zone out when he starts bragging.

My brothers are young enough to still get away with acting stupid, and they used to call me Biscuit. This was cute when I was five, but since everyone else abbreviates it to Kitty, I guess I should be grateful to them.

"You can crash at my place for a while," Joel offered, knowing that moving back in with my dad sat right at the top of a long list of things I did not want to do.

Since he sublet a shoe-box condo and dated a long string of ridiculously dimwitted girls, it was nice of him, but there was no way I'd take him up on that offer.

"Nah," I said casually. "I'll be fine. Dad and Janie will be happy to have us all under one roof again."

They absolutely would be. Super. Fucking. Happy.

Dad because then he could pretend that I was five again, and hence could pretend that I spent absolutely no time at all being more or less naked with anyone.

Janie because she's a bear, and her sole focus are on her cubs and her mate. Lucky for me, she claimed me right away as her cub. Or pup. Or cup... or whatever. And yes, she calls Dad her mate, which is sweet and ridiculous in equal measures. It also means we have to tell the few visitors finding their way to Nowhere that Janie is from Australia.

"You could stay with Fuchsia and the Az," Joel said, grinning widely and wiggling his brows to indicate that it was a joke.

As if that was needed.

From the first time they met, which unfortunately was whilst I was exiting detention, my mother and Joel disliked each other. Mom because she never seems to like anyone. Joel because she told him he looked like a carrot.

To her defense, she probably meant it as a sort of weird compliment because anything coming from nature is worshiped by the witches of Nim. Also, Joel did look a little like a carrot back then. He grew into his height though, and the longish red mohawk he keeps tied to the back of his head looks über-cool. Hence the string of silly girls chasing him around.

"Mom would alternate between moaning about my lack of ambitions and making me chant weird shit. The Az would offer me money to move out which is something I won't be able to say no to," I said. "And then I'll owe him."

"Not good," Elsa said. "Never good to owe a wizard in general. The Az..."

She trailed off because there really wasn't any need at all to share how not good it would be for me to owe that particular wizard anything at all. Ever.

"Right," I sighed. "Gotta go."

"They know you're coming?" Joel asked.

I shook my head and sighed again. "I'll surprise them."

My car started coughing out a clunky rattle as I drove out of the suburbs and when I was going up the mountain, it escalated to the sound of severe car-bronchitis. By the time I turned to my parents' driveway, it felt as if the car was skipping its way forward like a seven-year-old with a rope.

It died a quick death right outside the big brown double doors where a group of people was waiting.

Biff Brown. Janie Cameron-Brown. Bill, Joe and

Tom Brown.

And Hunter Brown. My darling and totally outrageous Grandpa.

What the hell was he doing there? And what was that on his head?

"Welcome home!" Dad shouted happily before my feet had even hit the ground. "Your room is ready and waiting."

Shit.

Pookie's owner would have called the police to help find her missing dog.

Dad was the sheriff. And not stupid.

My life truly sucked. Hugely.

CHAPTER 2

It'll be like summer camp

"Hey Daddy," I wheezed out as my ridiculously overprotective father squeezed me with his strong arms.

He smelled of the outdoors, and soap, with a little hint of last night's grill coming from his flannel shirt. The badge on his chest felt cold against my cheek, and I wondered if it'd leave a mark, just for a little while. That would probably please Daddy, who would have tattooed a big sheriff's star on my forehead if I'd let him.

Dad's official title was actually chief of police, but he'd early on in his career shared widely how using that title would be disrespectful to the Native Americans and that he was the goddamned sheriff and nothing else. I'd never figured out if Dad meant that as a joke or not, partially because Dad's closest friend, Robbie Blackbear, always chuckled and wiggled his brows when he heard it. Also, Daddy was a huge fan of old western movies in general, and Clint Eastwood in particular, so his wish to be called Sheriff Brown could come from a genuine desire to be like "the Clint." Either way, it didn't matter because Dad was elected to perform his duties, so it actually made more sense for him to be called sheriff.

The elected part of his appointment wasn't as much an election as the whole population of Nowhere county showing up at City Hall every four years to nod when Robbie Blackbear asked them if they wanted to keep Biff Brown as chief of police. Dad had a ten-year streak of zero unsolved crimes, and everyone wanted to move on to the whiskey-laced upside down cake Tina Blackbear made specifically for these events, so the whole thing usually took less than a minute.

Biff Brown was also the alpha of the local werewolf pack and had been since Gramps decided to retire twenty years ago. According to the lore among regular people, this should have involved a massive fight to the death between them, something that always made the wolves crack up because really? Why would we do something like that?

In reality, Gramps came home one day and told Dad, "Going to Florida for the winter, Son. You're it."

Then he left and spent the next three months soaked in raspberry margaritas, earning his living by singing Jimmy Buffet covers in a bar in Key West. I'm not supposed to know that he came back because of an angry husband or twenty, and a need for a hearty dose of penicillin. Both for Gramps and a few of the husbands apparently.

"You shouldn't have growled at that dog, sweetie," Dad admonished me gently.

"He shouldn't have peed on my leg," I retorted.

Dad stepped back to stare at said limb with a look of horror on his face, and I moved to the back of my car to get my bags.

"He -" Dad paused and tried again, "He peed?"

"I was standing there, minding my own business, texting Elsa. Pee. Leg."

My brothers were giggling like the stupid morons they were. Janie shook her head in disbelief, and Gramps barked out laughter.

"Jesus. Were there no trees around? Bushes?"

"I was in the park."

Another laugh came from Gramps, although it sounded mostly as if he choked on something.

"But you're a wolf," Dad said.

"Apparently Pookie missed the memo."

"Okay."

"Okay."

Since I didn't want Dad to say the words which so very clearly were at the tip of his tongue, I turned toward the porch and murmured casually, "Hey everyone."

"Welcome home, Kitty," Janie said with a sweet smile. "Dinner's ready in ten. Pork chops."

My casual smile turned genuine.

"Mashed potatoes, green beans, and gravy?"

"Of course."

Maybe it wouldn't be so bad to stay with my parents for a while, I thought. Rice Krispies and fast food had only been fun the first few weeks after moving out, and my cooking skills were nonexistent, to the point where I sometimes burned eggs when I boiled them.

"Hello there, Kitty my darling," Grandpa Hunter said. "You're moving in too, I hear."

Too? Gramps lived in the only apartment building in Nowhere, where most of the old folks preferred to spend their golden years. It was close to the stores and the small health care clinic, and they had the community center on the ground floor where they could meet and play Parcheesi or whatever else they did to amuse themselves.

"Lovely hat," I said instead of asking about his residential difficulties because I wasn't entirely sure I wanted to know what had happened.

"It's not a hat, silly. It's my skivvies."

I was neither blind nor stupid, so I'd seen that.

"Okay," I said, forcing myself to not ask about that either.

I was pretty sure any answer would be embarrassing, and I was not wrong.

"Keeping them warm," he said with a grin and an eyebrow wiggle I suspected he thought was lecherous. I could have told him that except for the drunken months in Florida, his time as a womanizer was over and had been for more than fifty years. The grin widened into a smile showing the gold teeth at the back of his mouth, and then he added, "Good for the balls."

"B -"

"Let's eat," Janie cut me off in a voice that was eerily calm. "Hunter. No headwear at my table, you know this. Boys, wash your hands. Mate, if you want a beer then go get it."

No one argued with Janie when she sounded like that. She might be five feet four and cute as a button, but she was still a bear, so we trooped inside and had dinner.

"Let me see if I got this right," Dad said, pushed his empty plate forward and leaned back.

Oh crap. I knew that voice.

"You got a job as a cashier at the supermarket. And got fired."

It didn't sound exactly like a question, but I nodded anyway. I could have told Dad that the old lady had been really offensive and totally deserved to have her cake smashed. Maybe not into her face, but that had been her fault. Completely. I'd meant to wiggle it a little, and if she hadn't leaned forward to poke me in the ribs, I would have put it down again.

"Then your mother set you up with that office-job," Dad went on. "I know," he cut me off when I wanted to protest. "It was a stupid thing to do, but Fuchsia has never been -" He cut himself off and winced, which meant Janie had kicked him in the shin. Hard. "Anyway. You got fired."

"Yes," I said.

The job had been one endless and mind-numbingly boring shuffle of papers, and there was no A/C in my small office in the basement. As a consequence, I mostly spent my days sleeping, leaning my head on the desk in front of me. Then the big boss walked in unexpectedly on a warm summer day to say hi to his dear friend Fuchsia's daughter, and I straightened just a little too quickly.

Having a paper stuck to my forehead kind of destroyed my chirpy greeting. And got me fired.

"You started college," Dad said.

Yeah. I totally saw where he was going with his reasoning.

"Yes," I snapped. "I got kicked out, okay. It's temporary, not my fault, and if you'd just let Joel do his thing I would have been let back in."

"Kitty," Dad said warningly.

I glared at him and was about to start yelling when a car came speeding down the gravel road. It was a spun sugary pink, and I knew exactly who owned that vehicle.

"Grandma Hazel!" my brothers squealed, and I was so happy my totally crazy grandmother was visiting that I didn't tell them how ridiculous it was for teenage boys to squeal. Or that Hazel was my goddamned grandma, not theirs.

I could do that later.

"Well this is quite a gathering," Hazel said and watched us as we lined up on the front porch. "Were you expecting me?"

Her black hair had started to change a few years ago, and she had immediately informed anyone who wanted to listen, and quite a few others, that she wasn't the least interested in any shades of gray unless they came with a hot guy who had millions of dollars, a joke she cackled loudly at even when nobody else did. Hot, gray-shaded guys with fortunes never seemed to enjoy my grandmother's overtures, though, and her current hair color was a pale purple, although it probably had a fancy name like "mauve spirits" or "lilac dawn."

"Of course we didn't expect you," Dad muttered.

"What was that, honey?" Grandma said breezily as if she hadn't heard every syllable.

"Why are you here?" Janie asked.

"I need my family around me in this difficult time," Grandma said quietly and put the back of her wrinkly hand against her forehead in a gesture which could not be described as anything other than fake drama.

Then again. Fake drama was probably Hazel de Chamontelette-Jones' middle name.

"What did you do?" Dad asked.

"Nothing."

"Hazel."

"A small mishap."

"Hazel."

Dad had to repeat her name a few more times, but she gave in eventually.

"The high priestess of Nim ordered me to scry because the Azdjakzian amulet is missing and I was apparently the only idiot available to look deeply into the pool of wisdom."

There was a long silence, and then I prompted her to go on.

"Mom ordered you to scry...?"

"Yes, Kitty darling. She did. And I did. The amulet is still missing, my house has burned to the ground, and..."

She trailed off, and her mouth quivered. Was she suddenly holding back laughter?

"What?" Dad barked.

"Fuschia got singed."

"Fuschia got what?"

"Singed."

"What does that even mean?"

"Oh, nothing dramatic. She's perfectly fine, Biff. She has no eyebrows right now, but they should grow back. I think."

The ensuing silence was deafening, but then Grandpa started laughing. When he did, my brothers did too. Dad tried his best to look serious, but the tips of his mouth twitched, and Janie turned abruptly to look at something inside the house.

"You think they will grow back?" I asked carefully.

My mom was very proud of her Nim-looks, and plucked her elegantly arched brows daily, I suspected.

"Absolutely," Grandma said. "I chanted words of healing almost immediately, and added a little extra oomph so they should grow back bigger and better than ever."

Oh God. My mother the Morticia Adams lookalike

with a unibrow.

"Why are you here?" I asked when the others just kept laughing.

"Fuschia is not so very happy with me at the moment."

This I could easily imagine.

"Uh-huh," Dad said noncommittally.

"I'm sure it'll pass, but I think that it would be wise for everyone if we were... separated from each other for just a little while."

"Uh-huh," Dad repeated.

"This is the one place where my daughter and son-in-law can't come."

She was right about that. When Mom forgot my birthday the first time, Janie got so angry I thought she'd tear down more than our garage. Then she told Dad that if my mother set foot on their land ever again, she'd rip off his private parts and shove them up a place on him where the sun doesn't shine. She used other words that were way cruder, and hair had been spouting all over her body, so Dad took her seriously. And Mom hadn't visited Nowhere once since that incident.

She still forgot my birthday every now and then, though.

"Of course you're welcome to stay here as long as you need, Hazel," Janie said.

Dad made a hoarse, rasping sound but kept quiet when he saw the look on his wife's face.

Janie smiled sweetly at him, and added, "Hazel, you're in the guest house. Hunter, you can take the apartment above the garage."

What? Wait, no!? I'd planned to stay in either of those. Janie knew what I was thinking, probably because it was written all over my face, and smiled just as sweetly at me.

"Kitty. I'm sure you'll be fine upstairs in your old room."

My old room. Right next to stairs which creaked in a way that made it impossible to sneak in if you by accident ended up coming home late. Or drunk. Or both.

Janie hadn't put it as a question, though, so I didn't bother answering.

"This will be great!" Hazel squealed. "It will be like summer camp."

I turned slowly and was about to growl at my grandmother for the first time in my life when a familiar scent hit my nostrils. I couldn't believe who apparently was approaching so I sniffed the air several times, and when my brain had accepted what my nose told me, I looked around to see where he was.

"Oh. Yeah, Kitty," Dad murmured. "I meant to tell you. Johnny Twoboats left, and I needed a replacement."

He hadn't hired...

"All of that crap happened a long time ago, sweetie," Dad said. "I'm sure you've both moved on by now."

... shit. He had totally hired him.

A tall man with blonde, wavy hair in a short

ponytail at the nape of his neck walked around the corner. He'd always been handsome, and the years since we last met hadn't changed that, so he still was. Disturbingly so. His features had sharpened, and he'd bulked up. A lot. When he saw me, his mouth widened into a lazy grin, and his gloriously blue eyes twinkled in a way I remembered well.

"Hey, babe," he rumbled, and his deep voice sent shivers down my spine.

Jackson Vik-Hansen was back in Nowhere.

"Kitty," Dad said quietly. "This won't be an issue."

I wasn't sure if he'd meant for that to come out as a question or an order, but I didn't care. I'd been around Hazel de Chamontelette-Jones my whole life, so I knew how to behave, and said with no small amount of breezy happiness in my voice, "Of course not. Why would it?"

Then I walked toward Jackson, the man who had been the boy who asked me to my high school prom. And canceled an hour before the event with the excuse that he had the flu.

"Hey, Jack," I said sweetly and made my own eyes twinkle as I let them slide over his gorgeousness.

When I was standing so close to him I felt his breath slide over my cheek, I used as much strength as the wolf-part of me could summon, and swiftly pushed my knee into his crotch. Twice.

"I told you!" Grandma exclaimed gleefully as Jackson went down, groaning hoarsely and cupping his groin. "Just like summer-camp!"

CHAPTER 3

Jackson Dick-Hansen

"Come on now, boy," Dad said calmly. "Up you go."

Jackson whined a little when Dad pulled him off the ground, and I smirked.

I'd whined plenty the night of my senior prom. At first, because I felt sorry for Jack who had come down with a severe case of the flu, and had sounded completely miserable.

By the end of the evening, the whining had been for other reasons.

Jackson Vik-Hansen had been the one all the girls chased after, and when he asked me to be his date I played it very, very cool... but squealed like an idiot on the inside. I'd looked forward to walking into the gymnasium with my hand in the crook of his arm.

Was that shallow? Hell, yes, it was. I'd known it

already back then and hadn't cared one bit because I'd never been cheerleader-in-the-movies kind of popular, so it had felt sweet to be asked by someone like Jackson.

Elsa, Joel and I were mostly ignored back in High School, although not in an unfriendly mean-girls-from-the-movies way. Between us, we mostly knew everyone, and we'd been treated with a fair deal of respect, but it had always seemed as if everyone kept their distance. Of course, my dad was Sheriff Brown, Joel was a widget and Elsa... well, let's just say that unicorns knew way too many secrets.

My prom night from hell probably hurt more than it should have because in addition to the shallow pleasure I felt when Jackson asked me, I'd also liked him. Not liked him as in sappy-loved him 'til the end of time. But he'd been cool, and we'd laughed a lot, so I'd... liked him. A lot.

"Are you okay, Jackson?" I asked in a voice full of fake concern.

"Uhnff," he grunted, and his knees buckled when Dad let go of him, but he managed to remain standing by grabbing hold of the porch rail.

"I'm so sorry," I went on. "You know I have a tic."

"Tic?" Grandpa asked.

"Yeah," I said and turned to grin at him. "My knee just starts bouncing when I'm too close to an asshole."

"Language," Janie snapped.

"Sorry," I said and did not mean it. "I meant when I'm too close to a lying moron."

"What is wrong with you?" Jackson asked hoarsely. "Wasn't what you did back then enough?"

No. It wasn't, not by a long shot.

"Kitty," Dad murmured, but I kept my gaze on Jack.

"She did some witchy crap that put pimples all over my as -" Jackson clamped his jaws together and amended his statement with a glance at Janie. "Sorry, Ma'am. Pimples all over my behind."

"They disappeared as soon as you cleared the county limits, didn't they?" I snapped.

We glared at each other, and the happy twinkle that had been in his eyes when he walked around the corner of the house was replaced with a steely look that I'd never seen before and didn't like. Then he moved one of his legs a little, let go of the porch rail and winced.

Maybe kneeing him twice had been overkill?

"Right," Dad said. "Jackson. I'm sure you want to check on things. You know where the bathroom is. Yell if you need an ice-pack."

"He can use my skivvies," Grandpa offered cordially, and waved his hand to indicate the boxer briefs that were back on his head. "They're nice and warm."

Jackson turned his head slowly to look at him, and the steely look faded away from his eyes.

"Thanks, Hunter, but there's no need."

"I can go with you," Grandma offered happily. "Help you check things out."

My eyes popped wide open, and I heard one of

my brothers snort out something unintelligible.

"Thanks, Hazel," Jackson said. "I think I'll manage quite well on my own."

When he turned toward Grandma, I saw that the twinkle was back in his eyes again, and it looked great on him.

Well, shit.

"Witches of Nim are excellent healers," Grandma pushed.

"I know," Jack said and looked at me. "This was the last shit I'll take for back then," he stated. Before I had time to come up with a suitably snappy reply, he leaned in close to my ear added in a quiet murmur, "Forgot how hilarious your family is, though."

Then he walked gingerly up the steps to the porch. We watched him in silence, and I decided that yeah. Kneeing him twice had totally been overkill.

When he was by the back door, he turned and grinned at me. And then he winked.

Winked.

After I'd pushed his nuts rather forcefully toward his tonsils and in front of my Dad. His alpha. And boss. Did he have a death wish?

When the screen door slammed shut, I turned to find my whole family staring at me.

"Kitty," Dad said sternly.

"Daddy," I said and fought the blush I felt creeping up my neck.

"Kitty," Janie echoed, although she sounded exasperated more than anything.

"That was harsh, Sis," one of my brothers said.

"Whatever, Joe," I said sourly.

"I'm Bill," he replied just as sourly.

I'd known that, but I loved messing with their heads and considered it suitable payback for all the shit they pulled on me.

"I get that he canceled your prom date, but the dude was sick. I don't think he -"

Hell no. I hadn't told them what actually happened, but I would now.

"The fucker," I said and speared Janie with a glare when she huffed at my choice of word, "called me and said he had the flu. I said I understood and promised to make soup for him."

Gramps started laughing, and I rounded on him.

"Chicken. Effing. Noodle," I snapped, and he laughed even more for some reason.

"Okay, sweetie," Dad murmured, clearly trying to placate me.

It didn't work.

"But there I was. I'd spent a gazillion dollars on my dress and hair, and I had put on makeup. I wasn't going to waste all that, and we had perfectly adequate cans of soup in the pantry, so I called Joel and Elsa. They picked me up, and I went to the prom with them instead."

They all knew this and were waiting for me to continue, but I paused for dramatic effect. I also needed to calm down because it felt a little bit childish to still be so pissed off.

"So?" Bill pushed when the silence lasted longer

than he was willing to wait.

"Guess who was on the dance floor when I got there?" I asked sarcastically.

"No?" Grandma Hazel wheezed.

"Who?" Gramps asked, and when everyone turned toward him, he added, "What? How the hell would I know who was at that prom?"

"Jackson Vik-Hansen," I stated. "And guess how far down Melissa Moose's throat he had his tongue?"

"No?" Grandma wheezed again.

"Two -"

"That was a rhetorical question, Hunter," Janie interrupted my grandfather's apparent attempt to guess the length of Jackson's tongue.

"Oh."

"Oh, yes," I confirmed. "Tongue in mouth, hands on ass, rubbing her crotch against his -"

"We get it, Kitty," Dad barked.

I was about to spew out more anger when the door opened, and Jackson stepped out on the porch.

"Everything seems oka -" He cut himself off when a rumble vibrated through the air. "What?"

The rumble changed into a low growl. My grandfather, father, and brothers were apparently not so pleased with him, and neither was Janie, but when I heard Hazel chant something under her breath, I decided enough was enough.

"Stop it," I said. "All of you. It's bygones. Jack can stay in Nowhere, just don't expect me to be happy about it."

Then I marched inside without looking back. The yelling outside started even before the screen door had closed behind me.

Excellent.

I sat down at the kitchen table and texted Joel and Elsa.

<Guess who's back in Nowhere?>

<Who?> Elsa replied within seconds.

<Yeah, who?> Joel chimed in immediately after.

<Who was the hottest guy in SHIT?> I asked back.

SHIT was the commonly used abbreviation of Saint Honoria of the Immaculate Transformation, which was the name of our old high school and also proof that the ancestor of mine who started the school more than a hundred years ago had humor.

I tapped my fingertips on the worn-down kitchen table as I watched the phone and waited for either of them to figure it out. Joel was the one who got it first.

<Jackson Dick-Hansen>

I laughed out loud when I saw his reply, and then we spent a good while coming up with other suitably insulting nicknames for Jackson. It was silly and juvenile, and it totally made my anger melt away. I loved my friends.

When we were done and had agreed that Fuckson Yuk-Hansen was the winner, the commotion outside had quieted down. The door opened slowly, and I looked up, expecting it to be Dad or Janie.

It wasn't.

CHAPTER 4

Yowza

Jack walked into the kitchen, and I let my eyes slide over his tall frame, telling myself it was to ensure that there hadn't been any injury inflicted by one of the five angry werewolves who had been growling at him outside. Or the bear. Or the witch.

He looked unharmed. I wasn't sure if that was a relief or a disappointment.

"I apologize for what I did," he said stiffly.

My eyes widened, but then I saw my father standing behind Jack, looking like a thundercloud. I suspected Jackson was close to a tragic wolf-mauling, as soon as he'd finished apologizing.

When the silence stretched out, Dad made an annoyed, huffing growl and nudged Jackson forward.

"Why did you do it?" I heard myself ask and could

have slapped myself.

I knew why.

Melissa Moose had been tall, blonde and built, and she might have been called "Loosey Moosey," but she'd been gorgeous. Slutty, but gorgeous. I had not liked her one bit even before Jack decided to lick her tonsils because she had also been catty and gossipy. She still was, when I thought about it.

"Jackson," Dad rumbled. "I think you owe my girl an explanation."

"You won't like it."

"Spill."

Jack sighed and kept looking at me.

"I was eighteen, alright?"

"I know," I said because I did.

"Eighteen and a boy and stupid. Only had one thing on my mind and I knew you wouldn't..." He trailed off, glanced at Dad and finished lamely, "provide that service."

Oh.

"So, yeah. I was stupid. Melissa called. Said if I ditched you, we would go at it all night. And I blew you off."

I blinked. It hadn't been because Melissa was prettier, or funnier, or that he liked her more. It hadn't been me lacking something.

"You ditched me so you could have sex with her?" I asked for clarification, needing to make sure that I'd heard what I'd heard.

"Eighteen," he retorted. "And a boy. She called and was pretty graphic in what we were going to do, so yeah. I did. And I'm sorry."

Huh. It had been a dumb thing to do, but it wasn't like we'd been a couple back then, so it wasn't as if he'd cheated on me. Exactly. He'd been an ass, but now I at least knew why.

"Okay," I said.

"Okay," he echoed.

"Boy," Dad barked, and Jack winced as he turned slowly. "You not trying to get in my daughter's pants back then is not a thing that makes me unhappy."

Of course, Dad would see it like that.

"Dad," I murmured.

He put his palm in my hand with a flourish that was not as much Clint E as it was Beyonce, but he kept his eyes on Jackson. And then he was suddenly grinning in a weirdly smug way.

"We're good for now. Stay out of Kitty's pants, and we'll stay good also in the future."

"Biff —"

"We're leaving," Dad announced cheerfully.

"Jackson," I said as they moved toward the door, and he turned. "Who says I wouldn't have... provided that service?"

Both men froze, and Dad wheezed out something, but my eyes locked with Jack's. His wolf must have been close to the surface because the blue deepened and a yellow glitter started to form.

"Guess you'll never know now," I added breezily and wondered what the heck I was doing, flirting with a wolf right in front of my Dad.

"Jesus," Jack muttered. "You gotta know what you

just said hurts more than the pimples you put on my butt."

"I know," I said with a grin. "Have a good time working with Dad, Jackson. Guess I'll see you around."

"Yeah," he sighed.

They left, and I stared at the door, completely unable to stop a ridiculous giggle to make its way up my throat.

I was so not a giggly girl, but that had been suh-weet.

Although, I hoped for Melissa Moose's sake that we didn't meet in the produce section of the supermarket any time soon. She would not look good with bananas shoved up her nostrils.

Janie and Grandpa joined me in the kitchen when a car started up outside. Janie's mouth was a thin line, and she went straight for the coffee maker, but Grandpa Hunter sat down opposite me.

"That was an okay apology, wasn't it?" he asked but didn't wait for a reply. "It was. Yes indeed. I took back my offer to lend him my briefs, but I shouldn't have done that. Not when he apologized so nicely."

He nodded with great satisfaction and the garment on his head bobbed a little together with his gray tufts of hair.

"Was Jackson angry?" I asked, wondering how the heck they had managed to get him to apologize at all.

Gramps misunderstood.

"Sadly, no. He wasn't upset at all and just growled that he doesn't use underwear and kept glaring at your father."

I froze. Jackson Vik-Hansen was apparently going commando.

Yowza.

"He's careless," Gramps went on.

Careless was not one of the words stumbling around in my head at that exact moment, although I wasn't going to share that, so I grinned at him instead.

He smiled back at me and explained, "It's important to keep your private parts warm, to ensure your reproductive abilities."

My grin faltered a little, and I blinked. Then I blinked again.

"You're not planning to, um, reproduce anytime soon, are you?" I asked.

"You never know," he replied.

You could have heard a needle drop in the kitchen, but then Janie put the pot back into the coffee maker with a rather unnecessary force. I couldn't for the life of me stop staring at my grandfather. His wrinkled face was serious, but there was a twinkle in his slightly faded blue eyes. The ash gray hair was a little too long, and I suddenly noticed a faint shadow on his jaw. Had he started to grow a goatee? At his age?

"They want my genes," he shared.

"Who?" Janie and I asked in unison, completely flabbergasted.

"Becky at the community center. Maybe Maria too."

"Buh..." I wheezed out.

The thought of Becky, who was four years older than me, wanting to do the mattress mambo with the man sitting in front of me with a pair of briefs on his head was disturbing on so many levels.

"Don't you think you're a little..." I tried frantically to come up with an alternative word to old because he was, but I didn't want to throw it in his face. After a few desperate seconds, I settled for, "Seasoned?"

Janie had still not said a word, but she suddenly started laughing.

"What?" I asked

"Seasoned, and also well done," she chuckled, shook her head a little and turned back to the sink. "Not going to happen."

"We have plans," Gramps said coolly and tapped his temple in a gesture that made him look like a crazier old coot than usual, which likely wasn't the effect he'd aimed for.

I almost squealed with relief when my phone started ringing.

"Heey!" I shouted without even looking who it was.

"That bad, huh?" Joel said with a chuckle. "Listen, Kitty. No time to talk now, but a buddy said they're looking for a bartender at Tiaso's."

"Tia-what?"

"Tiaso's. Biker bar just south of the city."

Say, what?

"You think I should apply for a job as a bartender?" I asked slowly, wondering if he'd gone insane.

Or maybe not. I had no experience being on that side of the bar, but if it were a biker place, then they'd mostly order beers or various shots. I could handle that. Maybe.

"It'll be fun. Ask if you get an employee discount."

"Wh –"

"Gotta go, sweetie. Hot date," Joel cut me off and disconnected.

I stared at the phone for a few seconds, and then I keyed in the name Tiaso's to see where the place was located.

"Kitty," Janie said in an infuriatingly patronizing voice.

I made my mind up immediately to get that goddamned job.

"Janie," I said, mimicking the tone of her voice.

"Your father will not be happy," she informed me, sounding as if this was a secret on par with the whereabouts of the holy grail.

"He might get away with yelling at Jackson, but I'm an adult," I said haughtily.

Our gazes held and then Grandma Hazel walked in.

She surveyed the scene, narrowed her eyes, and asked, "What's going on?"

"Kitty's going to be a bartender, and I'm thinking about procreating," Gramps answered cheerfully. "Janie is just a bit surprised."

"Fantastic!" Grandma Hazel squealed and slapped her hands together a couple of times in a sudden, and ridiculous, applaud. "Do you get an employee discount?"

She'd wisely ignored the procreation part.

"I don't even have the job yet," I murmured,

"What are you waiting for?" she asked. "Go get it. Tell them I'll be a regular."

I looked at my purple haired grandmother in her hippiesque dress which showed off her skinny-wrinkly arms, and the fact that cleavage was something one should cherish in one's youth because it went south with age. Far south.

I tried to picture her in a biker bar. I couldn't do it.

"I'll do that," I said instead. "My car died, can I borrow yours?"

She grinned happily and wiggled the keys in front of me, and when I saw the endless optimism in her warm, brown eyes, I couldn't hold my laughter back. Then I winked at Grandpa, got into the gigantic, pink car and drove down the mountain.

Tiaso's was undoubtedly a biker bar. This was evident from the long line of cruisers outside, although if someone didn't get it, then they could also just look at the orange neon sign in the window, alternately flashing the words "Biker" and "Bar."

I didn't stop to reflect on the wisdom in walking through the black door with another flashing sign that said, "Enter here," and I probably should have.

Inside, it was dark and smelled of beer, sweat, and motor-oil.

Yup. It was a biker bar alright.

The man behind the bar smiled widely at me in a

way I thought was a little too enthusiastic but running for the hills seemed like a wimpy thing to do, so I walked up to him and smiled back.

"Well, hello there, little girl," the man said

He was tall and had probably been muscular a long, long time ago. Now he was fat. And bald, although he had a surprisingly thick and slightly curly beard. He looked friendly, though, and his eyes were happy.

"Hey," I said with more confidence than I felt.

"Do you dance?" he asked weirdly.

I blinked, and he tilted his head toward the side a couple of times.

There was a small stage with a backdrop of red velvet.

And a pole.

Holy shit.

"Not really," I said.

My dad would blow a gasket if I got a job as a stripper, I thought. I also had zero desire to take my clothes off in front of an audience, and sub-zero desire when the audience would be the type of clientele scattered around the bar. They were Dad's age, more or less, and had the customary biker-attire of jeans, tees and leather vests. None of them were skinny, and all of them had some kind of facial hair.

"You sure?" the man asked.

I made a few deliberately awkward moves, entirely out of sync with Stairway to Heaven which was playing rather loudly.

"Shit," the man muttered.

"Heard you're looking for a bartender," I said with a smile that I hoped conveyed professionalism and not stripperesque sluttiness.

"Yeah?" he said and seemed to perk up. "You any good at that?"

"No clue," I said honestly because he'd figure out my lack of experience quick enough. Then I added calmly, "But I've been drunk plenty of times."

He watched me in silence and then a broad grin spread on his face.

"Fair enough," he said to my surprise, leaned behind the bar to pull out a bag. "Go put this on and get to it. I need a break."

A quick glance into the bag revealed something that seemed just slightly bigger than a handkerchief.

Well, crap.

"You still interested, girl?" the man chuckled.

"My name's Kitty," I said. "And I'll let you know by the end of the evening."

"Fair enough," he said again. "I'm Silenus. If you don't drink on the job and get through tonight without shoving a knife into someone's hand, then you have a job."

CHAPTER 5
The naked troll

"It was a goddamned handkerchief," I moaned. "Apparently one of the giants was sad about the loss of his puppy a few years back and drowned his sorrows with barrel after barrel of beer at Tiaso's. Forgot his hankie."

I'd been describing the thing Silenus had given me to wear, and Joel started laughing. I saw nothing humorous in this because the stupid thing had apparently become the mandatory uniform for all female bartenders at the bar. Which would be me.

The reason it was me was mainly the huge stack of bills Silenus had handed me at the end of the evening, saying that it was my share of the tips. I'd looked at the money, not entirely sure where it all had come from because the place had been half empty and most patrons had ordered the highly predictable beer and shot. Then I made a quick calculation in my head, grinned at Silenus and told him I wanted the job.

It wasn't actually that I wanted the job, as much as I needed the job. My landlord liked having a wolf in the building, and especially one related to Sheriff Brown, but he was unhappy about not getting paid. After some massive sucking up on my part, we'd made the deal that he'd hold the place for me for a month, after which I would have to give him the rent for three months in advance to get the place back. I hadn't seriously thought I'd manage, but if tips like the ones I got at my first night kept coming, I actually had a chance.

Elsa was either sympathetic to my situation, or kind enough to hold back her laughter.

"How do you even wear a handkerchief?" she asked instead.

"I altered it a little," I told her and grinned with satisfaction when I thought about the tear I'd made in one corner of the bright red piece of satin. "Cut one corner so I could tie it behind my neck. Tied two corners behind my back and the last one hung low enough to cover my crotch. Looked like a huge bib."

"Pretty sure it didn't," Joel snorted.

"Is it a regular place, or are there others?" Elsa cut in, and it was a relevant question.

According to the latest count, the world was mostly populated with regular humans. The term mostly was a slight exaggeration since the regular community was estimated to be fifty-four percent, but the universally agreed deal was that as long as the regulars were in the majority, we wouldn't confirm the existence of any others. As long as the regulars could vote to put restrictions on our kind, we'd just keep our mouths shut about it and let the regulars believe whatever the heck made them sleep well at night.

We could probably have told people about the unicorns, fairies or angels. Those guys had been very, very good at public relations. There was no way in hell anyone would tell anyone about werewolves or zombies, who had failed miserably at communicating the good deeds they did for everyone. It would probably freak the general population out to know that more than eighty percent of the staff at any police station was some kind of shifter. It was mostly wolves, or bears, though, with the odd puma here and there. The big cats usually preferred federal work, which dad numerously and scornfully had explained was solely due to the fact that they liked the "faggedy-suits" and the "assclown-haircuts." My dad was a jeans and tee man, who let his hair fall as it may after a shower, needless to say.

It would also not in any way be a good thing to share that virtually all teachers were zombies, although I suspected that to most high school students, this would actually not come as a major surprise.

"There are others in the bar," I said. "Some wolves. I spotted two fairies and a goblin. There's

LENA NORTH

something else too, but I have no clue what it is. Its scent was like; I don't know... booze?"

"It's a bar," Joel said, and that was a reasonable observation.

It wasn't what I'd meant, though, so I tried again. "Not like that, Joel. It doesn't smell like old beer. It wasn't icky. It was a scent of laughter and partying. Like drunken, hilarious times. It smelled like... fun?"

Elsa was frowning again, and I turned to her.

"Do you know what it is?"

"Might," she said slowly. "I'll come check it out."

Any shifter would have a good nose, even a half-blood like me, but unicorns had a unique ability to scent others and knew immediately what type of other they were. They also read auras, which meant someone like Elsa knew way too much about people, including how everyone honestly felt about anyone they'd ever met. She was scream-out-loud frustratingly discreet about it, though.

"Please do," I said, but felt the need to add, in case they hadn't understood, "You're going to look massively out of place in Tiaso's."

Elsa just shrugged daintily, which made her silvery dreads bounce a little, and murmured, "I won't mind."

Joel apparently minded and threw a rolled-up paper napkin straight in my face, and snapped, "Bikers like Disney princesses, Kitty. Like, a lot."

"That's what I'm afraid of," I shot back.

"Don't go there," Elsa warned us.

Elsa's cousin was so dull he could put people to

sleep just by breathing in their presence, which meant he was often mistaken for a zombie, but he wasn't a teacher at all. He was in the movie business, and Elsa didn't talk to him anymore. Not since the movie we weren't allowed to mention had hit the theaters.

I'd tried to tell Elsa that her cousin had used her looks and her name, but he'd at least not put her dreadlocks in the movie or made the princess a unicorn. Elsa wasn't budging. Joel had mumbled something about knowing a guy called Shrek and how he didn't have any problems with the movie he'd been put in, but that only made Elsa round on him, flaring her nostrils.

We'd both immediately, and wisely, started sharing how much we hated that dick-cousin of hers. Elsa was sweet, but when she was in her unicorn shape, she was friggin' big. I also found out early in our friendship that her two hind hooves could put one extremely uncomfortable bruise on each of your butt cheeks.

I was about to say something soothing when my eyes locked on a man walking down the street.

Did I say walking?

I meant sauntering.

No, stalking.

No, meandering.

No -

"Wow..."

Elsa had apparently seen tall, dark and handsome moving along the street as if he owned it. And the surrounding blocks. And the city. And -

"What?" Joel asked.

"Who is that?" I whispered reverently.

The man suddenly slowed down as if he'd heard my silent question through the window and across the street, and looked at me over his shoulder. As our eyes held, he grinned, and when he did, a golden glitter appeared in his black eyes. Then he turned and kept walking around the corner.

"Holy moly," I murmured.

"On a pogo stick," Elsa added.

"What," Joel snapped impatiently. "Good looking dude passing by, and you start drooling?"

"That was perfection," I murmured, still a little dazed by what I'd seen. "I wonder who he is."

"The question is, what he is," Elsa murmured.

"Get a grip you two," Joel ordered.

I was about to protest when a middle-aged, slightly overweight couple came walking right outside the coffee shop window. They suddenly stopped, and the man put both his hands on the woman's butt. Or, mostly on her hips since his arms were kind of short and he didn't reach all the way around her. Then they kissed.

"Holy shit," I said.

"I know," Joel said. "They're too old. Why don't they just get a room."

As if they'd heard him, they walked into the hotel next to the coffee shop.

"That was Benny's wife," I said.

"What?"

"Benny. He's at Tiaso's every night, sobbing in his beer about how his soon to be ex-wife is cleaning him out in their divorce."

"Is everyone crying in that place?"

I thought about it and shook my head.

"Not everyone," I said, but felt a need to be honest. "Although a surprisingly large number of bikers seem to be very in touch with their emotions."

"Yikes."

You could say that again.

"Come," I said and got up. "Benny is really sweet. Great tipper. We'll just take a peek next door."

The hotel looked nice enough, but they had their hourly rate listed next to the reception, which I guessed would bring their Yelp-rating down a notch. Or two. Or maybe not.

"Heey," I chirped to the young man half asleep behind the counter.

Great. A regular.

His eyes snapped open when he saw me, and even more when he noticed Elsa.

"Can I do you?" he asked.

"What?"

He cleared his throat in a way that sounded mostly like a squeak, swallowed and without taking his eyes from Elsa, he murmured, "I'm sorry. What can I do you for?"

"A million bucks wouldn't be enough for that, bud," Joel grunted.

"God, I'm so sorry. I meant, what can I do for you?" the poor dude said hoarsely.

"Which room did you give the couple who just walked in?" I asked.

He swallowed again, visibly.

"I'm not allowed to tell you."

Joel leaned forward and put his finger on the computer screen for a second. Having a widget friend was so fricking awesome.

"I didn't mean it like that," I said. "We'd like to check a room out, see if we want to rent one."

"Um," the man said.

"I'll stay here while you go and do that," Elsa crooned and peered at the poor receptionist man-boy through her lashes.

He immediately gave me a key and said, "Room four, upstairs," in another squeak.

Joel and I continued to the third floor, and he pointed at the room the couple would be in. I pulled out my phone and slammed my fist on the door a few times.

When the door swung open, I quickly snapped several pictures.

Then I realized two things.

They were both naked.

And the man was a troll.

"What the hell are you doing?" the man-troll grunted.

"Sorry," I said. "We'll just go."

He lunged at me, or my phone, but I turned and ran down the stairs with Joel at my heels.

"Get that camera!" the woman wailed, and I heard heavy steps behind me.

I saw the receptionist's wide eyes as I sprinted through the entrance but didn't stop. I did not do this on account of the naked troll coming after me at an alarming speed.

Three blocks up the road, he was still pursuing us. When I glanced over my shoulder, I saw that he was closing in, but accidentally lowered my gaze and got an eyeful of his lack of undies, so I squeaked and turned forward again, increasing my pace. His breath indicated that he was rather close to having a heart attack, but he was also a troll, so I knew he would never give up. He'd just keep going like a goddamned Duracell-bunny.

"Take this," I wheezed and threw Joel the phone. "Go left, I'll go right. He'll follow me."

Joel nodded, and turned around the corner, disappearing down the side lane as fast as his long legs could take him.

I kept running but I'd never been one to exercise much, and I was running out of steam. Since Joel had gotten away with my phone, I decided to stop and try to reason with the naked idiot.

The stupid troll ran right into me, and I toppled over. He did too, and we suddenly rolled around on the sidewalk. I tried to get away, but being a troll, he was also slippery, so I lost the fight almost immediately. He ended up on top, and I tried to move which unfortunately made him do what trolls usually did.

He sat on me.

I flailed my arms and legs, cursing profusely, but

he didn't move.

"Babe," a deep voice said next to us suddenly, and I stopped moving.

Well, crap. What were the odds?

"Is there a reason a naked troll is sitting on you?" Jackson Vik-Hansen said.

I could hear laughter in his voice and closed my eyes.

"No," I mumbled.

After that, my situation improved. Under the threat of getting arrested for indecent exposure and assault, the troll caved in and left us with a glare and a t-shirt Jackson got from his car. It was too small, and his sagging butt was visible beneath it when he lumbered off. I heard an older lady squeal when he rounded a corner, so I guessed it was too short in the front as well.

Yuk.

"What are the chances of you not telling Daddy about this?" I mumbled as I adjusted my clothes, trying to not get slime on my hands.

"Depends."

I froze.

"You gonna let me buy you a beer?"

I straightened and stared at him.

"You're blackmailing me into a date?"

"Totally," he said with a grin and a wiggle of his brows. "So, are we going out Saturday, or what?"

"I'm gonna have to go with; or what," I said haughtily.

Then I marched off, and it would have been a

fantastic exit from an incredibly uncomfortable encounter if I hadn't slipped in a what probably was a small glob of troll-mucus.

Jackson was laughing loudly as I crawled back up on my feet, trying to pretend that I didn't have my ass in the air and something both icky and sticky in my hair.

"Take a shower, babe. See you Saturday," he called out after me as I rounded the corner.

Well, shit.

CHAPTER 6

Date-night

It was Friday, and I had the evening off, and I had the evening off because I'd offered Silenus that I'd work the next night, which incidentally happened to be the Saturday when Jackson Vik-Hansen expected me to drink beer with him. Which I wouldn't. Because I would be working.

Ha.

My Friday-night plans mostly involved a tub of chocolate chip cookie dough and a movie where the main characters were idiots who misunderstood each other repeatedly but still kissed in the end.

I had a hate-love-hate-rinse-repeat relationship with chick-flicks that I was sure wasn't entirely healthy. I kept watching them, even though I groaned into a pillow for a significant part of the movie. Regardless of the level of groaning, I always sob-smiled as the happily-ever-effing-after unsurprisingly materialized in the end, feeling a little like when someone scratched me gently behind my ear.

Soothed. Comfy.

I'm part canine, what can I say?

I'd watch the movie with Grandma Hazel, who had offered to bring vodka. I wasn't sure hard liquor would go all that well with cookie dough, but one should try everything once, and it might, so I'd accepted the offer and told her to just keep it quiet around Dad who thought I still drank Virgin Marys. He thought I was one too. Not a Mary that is - the other thing.

"Hey, babe," Jackson said as I exited the house in a pair of yoga pants and one of Dad's black flannel-shirts, which really was the perfect outfit for dough-bingeing.

And vodka drinking, in my experience.

I yelped and glared at him.

"You have cologne."

"What?"

"You have some smelly stuff all over your neck, Jackson."

"Too much?"

It wasn't actually. I'd thought the scent I sensed had come from Dad's shirt and had cheered his deviation from a lifelong obsession with whatever-shit's-on-sale which usually was Old Spice.

It had hidden the scent of Vik-Hansen, though,

hence the yelp.

"Are you ready?" he asked when I didn't reply.

"For what?"

"Our date?"

I stared at him, and while I did this, my father stepped through the door.

"Hello, son. Good to see you here, and on time too. Excellent. Excellent."

I turned to stare at Dad instead, wondering if someone had slipped something into the coke he'd had with dinner. Or perhaps exchanged the mushrooms on his pizza for something slightly more exciting than champignons.

"Why do you sound jovial?" I asked and narrowed my eyes.

"I don't. I don't. Why would I?" Dad rambled happily. "Can't I greet my daughter's suitor on the porch in a friendly way?"

My what? He... what?

"Yoo-hoo," Grandma Hazel shouted and approached us from the guest cabin, crossing the gravel rather gingerly since she was teetering on high heels. "Jackson. So nice to see you, son. And on time too."

"What's going on?" I asked, when they simply stood there, beaming at me.

Yeah, okay, Jack wasn't exactly beaming because he was not a beaming kind of guy. He was grinning instead. Crookedly.

"We're going on a date tonight instead," Jackson informed me. "Talked to Biff, and he said you had to work tomorrow."

I turned my gaze to find him suspiciously blank-faced. Especially when one considered the humor in his eyes and how his tee moved a little around his belly which meant he was holding back laughter, but barely.

"Dad," I snapped. "I had a small incident with a troll. He was naked, and he sat on me, and Jackson is using that to blackmail me into a date."

There. Cookie dough and movie-night; You may commence.

"Oh-ho, son," Dad said, still in that weird booming voice. "Sneaky. Snee-kay-yay indeed." He turned to clap Jack on the back hard enough to kill any non-shifter, and added, "I might even say..."

Oh God, no, I prayed when he trailed off. Not a stupid dad-joke. Not now. Not ever.

"Sneaky like a wolf!"

Dad and Jackson laughed loudly, although Jackson did it mostly because of the look on my face. I was sure of this because the joke was so seriously unfunny there was no need for him to tilt his head back and laugh that way. It also made him look way, way too good.

"That wasn't funny," Grandma said.

"I think it was," Jackson said and winked at me. "Ready, Kitty?"

"We're totally ready," Grandma Hazel chirped.

"What?" Jack said, and his head snapped around so quickly toward her I wondered if he might have given himself a whiplash.

"You know how it works, son. Way of the wolves," Dad boomed. "Chaperone."

Yeah, that had totally been the way of the wolves. Like a thousand years ago.

"But -"

"You wouldn't try to take advantage of my young, innocent daughter, now would you?" Dad asked Jack, and the boom was gone from his voice.

"Not at all, bu -"

"Excellent!"

And there it was again. Boom. It might even have been louder than before.

My hysterical laughter was unfortunately taken as me agreeing to the date, and before I got a hold of myself, I was in Jackson's ginormous truck. Grandma Hazel was in the back, but she scooted to the middle and spent the ride leaned forward, chatting about everything from the weather to how Jack's grandmother really needed to stop giving me the evil eye.

Which she totally did, and it creeped me out, hugely.

Jackson gave in halfway into town, which was two minutes after we left Dad's property, and started chuckling. He still did when he parked the car. As we were in the process of getting Grandma Hazel out of the vehicle, another familiar voice called out.

"Kitty!" Grandpa Hunter came lumbering, without underwear on his head, luckily. "I told Biff I'd be happy to keep an eye on you youngsters."

He beamed at me so happily that I heard myself

saying, "That was nice of you, Gramps. Maybe next time?"

Jackson barked out laughter, which Gramps took as gratitude.

"Absolutely! We're having a karaoke night at the community center. You can come then," he said as he started walking again. "Have to go, hot date."

While we watched, he pulled out a baseball cap which he placed on his head facing backward. It was a little too small, so yeah. It looked kind of ridiculous.

"Karaoke night," Jackson murmured. "Won't that be fun, Kitty?"

I was about to start walking back to my parents' place when he deftly ushered us into Bubba's, which was the combined bar and post office in the village. He got me a beer without asking and handed Grandma Hazel a margarita.

Then we sat there, sipping our drinks in uncomfortable silence. I was sure as hell not making it easier for him, so I looked at the photos on the walls as if I hadn't seen them ever before. Which I had, and often because most of them were photos Grandpa Hunter had donated to add what he called, "Local color."

More like local lunacy, I thought when I spotted one I hadn't seen before. There was a group of old geezers in it, all holding one hand by their heads, thumb in their ears, and in the other, they held what looked like small shiny balls.

"So, Kitty," Grandma Hazel murmured between margarita-sips, apparently thinking that it was time to do her chaperone duties and get the conversation going. "What does a troll-penis look like?"

Jackson promptly snorted beer out through his nose. Some of it sprayed over the table, but most ran down his jaw, and he was so stunned he didn't even wipe it off.

I put my own beer down slowly and tried to figure out how to respond to that.

A weak, "What?" was the best I could come up with.

"Well I've never seen one," Grandma said innocently.

Jackson silently picked up the paper place-mat that was supposed to protect the table from Grandma Hazel's margarita and used it to wipe himself dry. It was red and green, and it left colored pieces of fuzz all over his face.

I decided not to tell him that.

"Let's not talk about that," I said to Grandma, who sank back in her chair, the picture of hurt innocence.

The silence stretched out again, and Grandma could apparently not let go of her curiosity.

"Just tell me, Kitty. Is it bigger than a wolf-pe -" she cut herself off when I snarled, and Jackson put the beer back on the table with a thud. "Okay, okay. No need to be testy. I'll just have to find out for myself."

Oh, for heaven's sake.

"It isn't bigger," I muttered.

"Really?" she squealed.

She was suddenly eyeing Jackson in a way that

made me wonder what else would come out of her mouth, and he saw it too.

"I bought a house," he said abruptly.

"A what?"

"A house."

"Where?"

"Here."

I looked around the room, and he started laughing.

"In Nowhere. Just outside town, other side from your parents. Fixer upper."

Understanding dawned.

If there was one thing my father liked more than the thought of his only daughter moving back to Nowhere and settling down, it was renovating the shit out of just about anything.

This meant that Biff Brown had taken one look at Jackson Vik-Hansen, ex-jackass who now was a police officer and the owner of a fixer-upper, and yelled, "SON-IN-LAW-MATERIAL!"

Hopefully, he had either yelled very, very silently or in private. Perhaps he'd held it in until he was in the rest roo -

"I was there," Jack murmured.

"What?" I asked, hoping to God he hadn't read my thoughts.

"When he yelled, babe."

Our eyes met, and he grinned.

And he looked good doing it.

Crap.

CHAPTER 7

Jesus

"I'm working," I said into the phone and listened to the sounds of silence my mother produced while she processed this simple sentence.

Okay, so I wasn't exactly working, but I was on my actual way to Tiaso's when Mom called, and I took that as fate sharing with me that I could avoid having an extended conversation with her, something that never ended well. At least, never for me.

"Working?" she said in a way I found slightly insulting because it wasn't my first job.

It was actually my twenty-third, but that was entirely beside the point.

"Yes," I said, and added, "Mom, I'm so sorry, but I really have to go."

I'd gone for syrupy sweet and figured my voice

had hit just the right note.

"You wouldn't lie to me, Hibiscus?"

"Of course not, why would you think that?" I asked.

I was totally lying to her, but she didn't know that. It was also every daughter's responsibility to lie to their mother at least once every day, wasn't it?

"Maybe because I'm standing next to your car?" she asked, and I turned my head slowly to look straight at the Az' crotch.

"Yikes," I squealed and whipped my head around to the other window so fast I dropped my phone.

Yes. There she was.

I rolled down the window and smiled politely at her. The politeness wobbled a little when I saw her eyebrows. They were only half grown back, so they were stubby, and it was not an attractive look.

"Hey, Mom," I said. "Look, I really have to go. I start working -"

"Step out of the car," she said.

I stepped out of the car.

"Hello, Hibiscus," the Az said and raised one brow.

It looked really ridiculous, mostly because I'd had an urgent need after downing four cans of Fanta when I was six and ran into the bathroom to find him practicing it. I'd laughed so much I'd had to change my underwear, something he had been less than appreciative about. Both the panty-change and the call he had to make to his butler to ask him to tell their housekeeper to send one of their maids to mop the floor.

"Hello, Aïdan," I said sweetly.

His mouth tightened in anger, but honestly, if he didn't want to be called, "A-ee-dan," he should remove the diaeresis mark and spell his name Aidan like a normal person.

"Have you talked to your grandmother?" Mom asked.

"Yes," I said because I had indeed talked to my grandmother many times in my life.

"What did she say?"

I blinked and wondered what they were up to.

"She asked me what a troll-penis looks like," I shared.

Mom blinked, and the Az huffed out some air, but they didn't respond to this, which actually was quite understandable. I hadn't known what to say either.

"Look, Mom," I said. "Just tell me what you want, please. I don't want to be late for work."

"Hazel needs to help us find something that has been misplaced," the Az drawled.

"Stolen," I corrected him. "She told us."

"Hibiscus," Mom snapped. "The Azdjakzian amulet can't be lost."

"Why?"

They stared at me, and I shrugged. I had not been entirely awake during some of the which-classes I'd had to take, and this seemed to have been covered in one of those.

"If used the wrong way, it will crack the Cascadia fault wide open."

Okay, yeah. That was actually a pretty big deal.

Movements in the Cascadia fault would mean earthquakes and other shit so I could see how finding that amulet sooner rather than never would be a good thing.

"I'll ask Grandma to scry," I offered.

"Now," the Az said.

"I'm working tonight," I said. "I'll ask her tomorrow."

"Tell her there's a reward offered by the Wizard's Council. One million dollars to anyone who finds the amulet."

"I'll tell her," I said, knowing that Grandma Hazel couldn't care less since she owned half of Wisconsin. Or Wyoming. Or Winnipeg. Something with a W. "Have to go now, but I'll call you, Mom."

Then I got back into the car and got the hell out of there.

I had to call Joel and ask him to do his thing, which he did, so I had green lights all the way through town, and walked into the bar with two minutes to spare.

It was a slow evening for being a Saturday, so I had time to think during my shift. It also wasn't a job that anyway required extraordinarily high brain activity since the orders were either a grunted, "Beer," a friendly, "Beer and a Jaeger, babe," or, "Give me a shot of the strongest shit you have." The strongest shit also meant Jaegermeister, I'd discovered, and had learned the hard way that when they said it like that it was a good idea to hand out quadruple napkins and keep them coming. The napkins, that was.

My thoughts that evening kept circling back to the night before and the date with Jackson, and it did that stupid circling because we'd actually had a good time.

Except perhaps when the owner of the bar, who incidentally also was Jackson's uncle, had told him to wipe the fuzz away from his face, sharing with Jack that he looked like, "A fucking Christmas tree." Jack had not found that nearly as hilarious as I did.

Or when Melissa Moose walked in and sat her fat ass down at the table next to us. She hadn't stayed long, though. The fern hanging in a clay pot next to her had started slapping her in the face repeatedly, so she left with a sour look at me, which was unfair because that was not something I knew how to do. I might have given the door a little extra oomph though, but how was I to know that it would slap her in the back, making her stumble on the doorstep and fall flat on her face. Her nose hadn't been broken, so her whining had been a little over the top if you asked me. Which no one did.

I'd tried to thank Grandma Hazel for the fern-bitch-slap before Jackson came back from shoving rolled up paper napkins up Loosey Moosey's nostrils, but she waved it away with a breezy, "Pooh."

Then Jackson returned, carrying two more beers and laughing so hard he almost dropped them. Grandma looked at him and then at me. And then at him again.

"I'll just go talk to the very nice-looking bartender for a while," she chirped. "It will give you some time to kiss a little, or talk about the size of his private parts, or whatever."

I'd stared at her back and closed my eyes.

"I'm guessing you don't want to know the size of my -"

My squeak cut him off.

"Kiss?" he asked.

I wished he'd sounded a little more hopeful and a lot less like he was laughing at me.

"I think we should go with whatever," I mumbled.

We'd ended up talking about the place he'd had down in Salem, and how he was working around the clock to renovate one of the bathrooms in his house since this apparently was the roadblock to him moving in.

"I refuse to shit outside," he shared.

I stared and him and told him the obvious.

"But you're a wolf."

"Yeah, well, most of the time I'm not, babe. It's not like I'm gonna step outside and squat like a fucking moron."

Before I could come up with a witty retort, Grandma Hazel came back.

"I got his number," she stage-whispered and waved a small piece of paper.

There was absolutely nothing to say to that either, and since Jackson apparently shared that sentiment, he took us home instead.

For some reason, I'd said that I might go on another date with him. Maybe.

Crap.

"Hey, Kitty," a thin, wily-looking man greeted me, and I smiled widely, glad for the distraction.

"Benny, hey," I said and reached for the beer I knew he'd want. "Got something for you."

Then I gave Benny printed copies of the pictures I'd taken of his wife and the troll and promised to email him the originals. He stared at them for so long I started to worry, but then he howled.

I winced. If you aren't a wolf, you really should avoid howling.

"You just saved me close to a million dollars," he shouted.

Huh. Benny was apparently loaded, but the foxes usually were, so that wasn't exactly a surprise.

"Here," he said, and I stared at the big pile of cash he held out toward me.

"There's no need to -"

"I've paid a PI four times that and he came up with nothing. Now I can cancel that contract, so you earned it."

Okay. If he put it like that, I wasn't going to object, so I didn't.

I was tucking it into my pocket when something hit me. It wasn't a scent. Or a sound. It felt like a soft wave of warmth washing over me, and I straightened.

Tall dark and handsome had entered the bar and walked straight up to me.

"Hey, babe," he said.

His voice felt like warm honey sliding over my skin, and my step-mom was a bear, so I totally knew how that felt.

"Jesus," I whispered.

His mouth widened in a smile and glitter started to form in his eyes.

"That's my cousin," he said calmly. "I'm Rafael."

My racing mind came to a screeching halt.

He couldn't be a cousin to the actual Jesus Christ, could he? There were many kinds of others around, but still. No. Of course not.

"I'm -"

"Kitty," he cut me off. "Let's go."

Let's go? Was he nuts? Gorgeous, but nuts. Mostly gorgeous, when I thought about it, but still.

He had started to walk away but turned and frowned at me when I didn't move.

"Let's go," he repeated a little more forcefully

"I'll pass," I said.

He walked back through a room that suddenly was silent and stopped in front of me with a frown.

"You'll pass?" he asked slowly.

"I have a sub-zero desire to walk away with a complete stranger in the middle of my shift," I shared. "So, yeah. I'll pass."

He watched me for a while, but then he smiled.

"You just became a whole lot more interesting, Kitty Brown," he said.

I was not at all sure this was a good thing.

When Silenus suddenly started laughing, I suspected that it was, in fact, a very bad thing.

"So, Kitty. Tell me about yourself," Rafael murmured.

"No," I replied and walked away to hand Benny another beer.

Silenus laugh turned hysterical.

Rafael frowned.

Benny was grinning like a fool when I handed him the beer.

What the hell was going on?

CHAPTER 8

An electric blue speedo

I was sitting in a deck chair, sipping pink lemonade and munching idly from a big bowl of popcorn as I watched my grandmother scry. Don't get me wrong; it was something I'd seen tons of times before, and it wasn't as if it was a huge source of entertainment, but it was Sunday, and I had nothing better to do.

Grandma Hazel sat calmly in her circle, staring into a plastic bowl filled with water and mumbling witchy words of encouragement. Every now and then she winced or twitched, and then she grinned.

"What's with the grin?" Joel murmured next to me.

"How would I know?" I asked.

"Maybe because you're a witch too?"

"Only half," I mumbled and shoved more popcorn

into my mouth. "And they wouldn't let me scry."

"Remind me again why you let that stop you," Elsa said sleepily.

The sun was out, and she sighed a little as she leaned back and closed her eyes again. Unicorns were not good in direct sunlight, even in their human shape. Elsa had explained that it was somehow related to the fact that they glittered.

"Scry the wrong way, and you'll release all kinds of shit."

"Huh," Joel said and nabbed some of my popcorn.

"Hey," I snapped. "Eat your own. It's like you don't want your share of the cash I got from Benny," I added, but put the bowl down and pulled out the pile of money.

They both straightened and stared as I started splitting it up into three piles. Then I handed them one third each and grinned.

"I see a night on the town coming our way," I shared.

"I see a return to your place coming your way," Joel said and put the cash back on my lap.

"Don't need it," I protested. "I have half of what I need already. Last night was weird but highly profitable."

"Great tips?"

"Beyond," I said and turned back to look at grandma who had started swaying a little from side to side.

That was an understatement, actually. I'd thought Rafael would leave, and had looked forward to watching his back as he walked out the door, and not only because his buttocks were each like a priceless work of art. The way he kept his eyes locked on me had been unnerving, and it had taken most of my energy to keep smiling blandly.

Instead, he planted his fantastic ass on a stool and started chatting with the other customers, most of whom he seemed to know surprisingly well. Now and then, someone would ask for a drink, and when they did, they handed me enormous tips which I apparently deserved for being entertaining.

"I'll stop by Tiaso's tomorrow," Elsa said. "The place seems like fun, and I want to meet sex-on-legs."

Joel scoffed, and I turned toward him.

"If you didn't like girls so much, you'd get it." I thought about that for a while and added, "He might make you gay, actually."

Joel grinned at me and shared that he'd come and see for himself.

"I got it!" Grandma Hazel shouted.

I got up and reached for my phone, knowing that Mom was waiting for news, watching her own phone, tapping her fingers on the table next to it and arching her carefully groomed, albeit stubby brows.

"Where is it?"

"Where is what?" Grandma asked. "Oh, yes. The amulet. It's shrouded in secrets and whoever has it didn't want me to see."

I blinked.

Grandma Hazel grinned.

"I knew he'd made a mistake," she said.

"What are you talking about?" I asked slowly.

"That nice looking bartender at Bubbas," she explained, sounding as if I'd taken a trip down the slow lane. "I called him yesterday, but he'd given me the wrong number by mistake, so I ended up at a car-wash all the way over in Hillsboro."

Oh, God.

"Um, Grandma," I said, ignoring the suppressed laughter from my less than helpful friends. "It probably wasn't."

"Wasn't what?"

Could she be that naïve?

"I'm pretty sure he didn't give you the number by mistake."

"He could have seen my car, and it does indeed need a wash."

Yes. She could apparently be precisely that naïve.

"Grandma Hazel," I murmured. "I do it all the time. Fugly dudes, or whatever dudes that I don't want to see again... I give them the number to Marcobelli's Pizzeria."

Understanding hit her, and she turned to Elsa and Joel

"The dean's office at Reed," Elsa said laconically.

"Environmental Protection Agency," Joel murmured.

She stared at us, and then she started laughing.

"Hilarious!" she squealed. "I will have to go back to Bubba's. I only called to let the poor dear know I'm not interested. You know? In case he was waiting by the phone."

I made a mental note to call Bubba and tell him to warn the staff about her upcoming visit.

"What about the amulet?" I asked.

"I only got that it was old, which I knew. It's involved with something small, or it could have been many small things. The dwarves might have it? Or the brownies?" She thought about it for a while, and added, "Someone was naked, I think, so it's probably the brownies who have the amulet. Dwarves are never naked."

"I'll call Mom," I sighed.

"Tell her I'll try again," Grandma Hazel said. "No need to tell her about –"

"I won't," I assured her, wondering why she'd entertain the idea that I'd share with my mother that her mother was unsuccessfully trying to pick up young bartenders.

"Hello everyone," a loud voice boomed behind me, and I turned.

"Hey, Gramp –"

The rest of my sentence came out as a hoarse, gurgling sound through a mouth that had fallen wide open.

Grandpa Hunter had walked out on the porch with two of his friends. Wearing only a pair of electric blue Speedos. His friends' outfits were lime green and leopard print respectively.

I closed my eyes and wondered just how much bleach I'd need to pour in my eyes to erase the sight of three men in their dotage wearing trunks which I was pretty sure flossed their butts, regardless of whether the manufacturer had intended for them to do so, or not.

"I went for the biggest version, and I think the ladies will like it," Grandpa Hunter said. "Or?"

My eyes flitted down to look at the garment because it hadn't seemed that big to me. Then I squealed and closed my eyes again.

His crotch was huge. Like, enter the door five seconds before he did, huge.

I'd heard my father brag about swimmers and his ability to produce triplets for as long as I'd lived but he'd refrained from discussing dimensions, which would just have been plain wrong. I was suddenly even more grateful for his restraint.

"Say again?" I asked when no one said a word and Grandpa just kept grinning.

"Found it on the internet," he shared. "It's nifty. You tuck your willy inside and bada bing."

He made a sweeping movement in front of his crotch.

I promptly did what any girl would do at such a moment.

I opened my mouth and screamed, "DAD!"

My father came rushing through the woods and reached us at my fifth shriek.

"What's wrong?" he shouted.

Then he caught sight of Grandpa, and his rush came to a screeching halt, which made Jackson run right into him. Not even Jack's big frame could apparently move dad out of his frozen stupor, and

Jackson ended up plastered to his back, watching the spectacle on our porch over dad's shoulder like some weird ventriloquist-doll.

"Wha…" Dad said, swallowed, and tried again, "Wuh?"

He was apparently not stunned into silence but at the same time not able to verbalize his astonishment, which was understandable considering the sight in front of him.

"What do you think, Son?" Grandpa Hunter asked amicably. "Looks nice, huh?"

"Can I touch it?" Grandma Hazel breathed.

"No!" Elsa, Joel and I shouted.

A scuffle ensued during which dad got the story out of Grandpa. Grandma Hazel butted in, and the other two gentlemen helped explaining how the contraption worked. They had apparently thought it prudent to purchase a slightly smaller version, something I took their word for. Wolves were usually pretty hairy creatures also in their human shapes, and I feared seeing a minuscule, leopard print Speedo surrounded by tufts of gray hair would be the fastest way to have an actual stroke.

During the commotion, my brothers had appeared from nowhere, and then the screen door slammed. And I exhaled.

Salvation had entered the fray in the form of my step-mother.

"Janie," I whimpered. "I can't do this. You have to do something, or I will find the closest bordello."

"What?" Dad barked.

"I think I could be a highly successful hooker, Dad," I whispered. "That will easily give me the rent money I need. You always said I didn't spend nearly enough time on my homework and way too much time on my back, so I'd just –"

Dad was suddenly roaring, my brothers were snickering, and both Joel and Elsa were laughing so hard they had to lean on the house.

My eyes met Jackson's, and he was grinning crookedly.

"You have got to let me take you on another date," he murmured.

"If you're looking for a nice bordello, there's one just ten miles away that seems to be above average," Grandpa cut in, and his friends nodded. "The girls are really friendly. I can give you the address."

"What?" my father barked again.

"We had to make sure everything was in working order."

Everyone went silent.

"I'm not sure if you're aware that solicitation is a crime, Hunter?" Jackson asked quietly, but I could see the tips of his mouth quivering, so I figured he wasn't planning to arrest Grandpa anytime soon.

That was probably a good thing because jail time in that outfit would not end well for Gramps.

"Of course I know that, Jackson. I used to be the chief of police, remember? We didn't do anything," Grandpa shared jovially.

"We just took a look at the ladies. Wanted to make sure everything was twitching and shaking the way it's supposed to," the lime green speedo-clad man explained, just as jovially.

I groaned.

"Right," Janie snapped. "Hunter. Take your friends inside, get out of the false advertising and get dressed. Hazel, call your daughter to let her know what you found out. Biff and Jackson, go back to whatever you were doing. Boys. Either you disappear, or you're on laundry duty for a month."

Everyone started moving, but I heard Grandpa mutter something about it not being false advertising. Janie heard too and stomped her foot. The three old men suddenly looked at each other and grinned. Then they put their left thumbs in their ears and wiggled the fingers, and their brows. I stared at them, which I shouldn't have done because they turned, and I accidentally got a good look at their elderly backsides.

Yikes. I'd been right about the flossing.

"The bathroom is done," Jackson murmured into my ear.

"What?" I breathed, still a little stunned by the sight of an electric blue string disappearing between my grandfather's butt cheeks.

"You could come over to my house and try it out," he murmured and moved a few strands of hair away from my shoulder in a way that made a shiver run down my spine.

I looked into his blue eyes, and he winked at me, but then his words penetrated, and I blinked.

"You're asking me to come and poop at your

place?"

His eyes started laughing, but he said calmly, "Or pee. You don't even have to tell me which option you pick."

He moved some more hair to tuck it behind my ear, which caused another body-shiver, and I heard Elsa giggle.

Then my phone rang, and I grabbed it with a desperation I was pretty sure wasn't attractive, but the events which had just passed on my parents' porch had been unsettling, to say the least.

"Hey," I chirped, hoping that it wouldn't be my mother, but willing to talk to anyone at that point.

"Hello, angel-face," a deep voice murmured.

Rafael.

CHAPTER 9

Just another evening at Tiaso's

"Hey," I said, trying desperately to sound casual in spite of my confusion.

How the hell had Rafael found my phone number? If Silenus had given it to him, I'd figure out a spell that made his beard turn blue.

"Bad time?" he asked, and I could hear laughter in his voice.

Talking to Rafael with Jackson standing so close I could feel the warmth of him through my tank top was pretty uncomfortable, but I wasn't going to tell either of them that.

"Why are you calling?" I asked instead.

"Is that wolf there?"

"Which wolf?" I asked.

There were five curious wolves on the porch with

me. And one of them looked seriously pissed off, something I wasn't planning to tell Rafael either.

"The one with the cutesy ponytail who looks like he bench-presses Buick's and should be on the cast for Vikings."

Jackson growled. Damned wolf-ears.

"Ah," Rafael murmured. "He heard that?"

"Why are you calling?" I asked again, trying not to laugh at his ridiculously apt description of Jack.

"I have a job for you."

I blinked.

"I already have a job," I countered.

"This is just a teeny little thing. More a favor than a job, in fact. Just a friend of mine who needs to find this thing he misplaced."

I blinked again.

"No," Jackson snapped, leaning forward to speak into the phone which meant his mouth was about an inch from mine.

And he didn't move back.

"He decides what you can and can't do?" Rafael murmured smoothly.

Jackson's eyes locked on mine and it didn't take a mind reader to figure out that he wanted me to tell Rafael to get lost.

So, of course, I said, "I'd be happy to help. Let's talk about this tomorrow."

"It's a date. Tiaso's at nine."

Jackson growled again, but I growled right back. Rafael started laughing.

"I'll be there," I chirped.

Then I hit the screen to close the call and put the phone in my back pocket with what I hoped was an air of nonchalance.

"He calls you angel-face?" Jackson snapped.

"That is so cute," Grandma Hazel cut in, stepped back with her hands in the air when Jackson glared at her, and added defiantly, "Well, it is."

"Hey, Jackson," Elsa said. "Long time, no see."

"Huh," was the only answer she got.

"Jack," Joel murmured. "Welcome back."

He didn't get any answer at all.

"Okay," I said breezily. "I'm going to call Mom now."

"Kitty," Jackson said quietly.

"What is the matter with you?" I snapped. "He's like two hundred forty-five years old, and he had a job for me."

Okay, that was a massive fib. So massive it wasn't even a fib but an outright lie, but Jackson didn't know that, and since my dad had started to scowl, I figured it was justified.

"Who was that?" Dad grunted.

"One of the customers at Tiaso's," I said, and that wasn't a lie. "One of his friends had misplaced something. They probably just wanted me to look in the lost and found box at the bar."

And with that, I was back to fibbing again.

"Can I call Mom now?" I snapped, ignored everyone and walked away.

For the first time in my life, a conversation with Fuchsia de Chamontelette-Azdjakzian was preferable to what I was doing.

***

The bar was full of people, and I was busy pouring eight Jaeger-shots for a group of dwarves and their lady-friend when Elsa and Joel walked in. As expected, every goddamned burly dude in the entire place shifted their gazes from the dark-haired girl hanging with the dwarves, straightened and started grinning.

Those biker boys sure liked their Disney princesses.

Elsa walked through the place seemingly oblivious to the attention she was attracting. When she and a grinning Joel reached me, a couple of men immediately offered her their seats with a slightly embarrassing flourish.

"Thank you," she said sweetly.

Joel took the other seat which earned him a frown.

"Hey, Kit," he said, ignoring the biker-glares. "Beer?"

I nodded, finished pouring the shots and got my friends their drinks.

"He's not here yet?" Elsa murmured.

"It's ten to nine."

She didn't respond, and I recognized the slightly vacant look on her face, so I walked over to fill up an order from one of the waitresses. That would give her time to scan the bar and figure out what kind of other everyone was.

Five minutes to nine the door opened again, and my grandmother walked in, followed by my grandfather and a man I'd last seen wearing lime green speedos. He was now in baggy chinos and an equally baggy wife-beater, which was an improvement, albeit just barely.

"Yoo-hoo," Grandma squealed and pranced through the place as if she was on a garden party with her fellow Nim-witches. "Can I have a Margarita?"

I turned to Silenus who had frozen and stared as if in a trance at the tall, willowy woman wearing a long, flouncy dress in various shades of turquoise, and whose newly colored hair was a rather aggressively bright pink with white highlights.

"Grandma," I murmured.

He started grinning.

"Welcome," he boomed. "What a lovely surprise. I will make you the best Margarita you've ever had."

Two minutes to nine, Jackson walked in with my three brothers.

Or, yeah. Let me rephrase that.

Just before Rafael arrived, an overbearing, wolf-shifting police officer walked into my place of work together with my moronic and also underage brothers.

"For fuck's sake," I muttered under my breath and handed Benny his requested beer and shot.

Joel turned and started grinning.

"Pretty sure this will be fun," he said with no little amount of glee in his voice.

I was about to take a break that lasted the rest of the evening when Jack and the idiots reached me. And the door opened.

Rafael walked in, paused to stare at the gathering in front of me, and promptly started laughing. His black eyes glittered with humor, and the way his long hair swayed was mesmerizing. It sounded as if one of the bikers had punched Elsa in the stomach and Joel muttered an affirmation that he might in fact bat for the other team if this dude was playing too.

"Oh, wow," Grandma Hazel squealed, and I was about to agree with her when she added, "This has got to be the best Margarita in my life!"

"Told you so," Silenus crooned.

He was leaning over the bar and grinning in a way that could not be described as anything other than salacious. Grandma Hazel was also smiling and then she blew him a kiss. He pretended to catch it and press it to his heart. Or, press it to the top of his enormous belly, at least. I shuddered.

"I thought you said he was two hundred forty-five years old," Jackson suddenly said.

I closed my eyes.

"I'm not that old," Rafael murmured, and I opened my eyes to look at the two men in front of me.

For the first time, I regretted snoozing during witch-class because I distinctly remembered someone droning on about a spell that made you invisible, something which would have come in incredibly handy at that exact moment.

"I'm two hundred thirty-eight. And four months."

My mouth fell open, and I turned to Elsa.

"He's a vampire?" I whispered.

She shook her head, sniffed a little and her eyes widened.

"We'll talk later," she whispered back.

"I want to know now," I protested.

"It's complicated."

"You do realize we can hear you?" Jackson said exasperatedly.

"Do you wear underwear?" Grandpa Hunter cut in.

His voice was somewhat loud, and all conversations in the bar stopped abruptly.

"What?" Rafael asked when he realized that it was his wardrobe choices the old geezer was inquiring about.

"Jackson here is living dangerously. He does not wear briefs. How about you?"

There is was. My moment to close my eyes and never, not ever open them again.

"I live for danger too," Rafael said.

I forgot my vow to keep my eyes closed. They flew open, and I found myself staring straight into a pair of black eyes full of laughter. I turned mutely to look at Jackson.

"Perhaps you could arrest Grandpa Hunter?" I suggested weakly.

"On what grounds?" he asked calmly.

"I don't know, Jack. You're the cop. Harassment? Attempted murder?"

Jackson blinked and asked, "Murder?"

"If he asks me about my lack of underwear, I will die."

And there the bar went silent again.

"That came out wrong," I shared. "I wear panties."

"Okay," Jackson said.

"You sure?" Rafael asked and wiggled his brows.

"Of course, I'm sure," I snapped. "They're black lace, and the edges itch my –"

Jackson started coughing, Rafael began to laugh, and so did Joel and Elsa.

I tried my best to not blush and cleared my throat.

"Does anyone in this goddamned bar want another beer?" I shouted at the top of my lungs.

Hands went up everywhere, so I ignored the situation at hand and got to work. In the corner of my eye, I saw Jack and Rafael eye each other suspiciously, and then Jack said something. Rafael straightened, and I tried to hear what they said, but I only caught snippets because I also had to keep an eye on Grandma Hazel who had a gathering of old men around her, and Grandpa Hunter who was talking to one of the biker babes about how to best groom a goatee. Since the biker babe wasn't as much babe as she was biker, her own goatee was quite impressive.

When there finally was a lull in the requests for

drinks, I walked over to Joel and Elsa and bugged my eyes out at them.

"Help me," I hissed. "I don't know what to do."

"You should be careful, Kitty," Elsa said. "Sex-on-legs is an –"

"Kitty," sex-on-legs himself called out. "Come here."

I turned slowly and shook my head. Elsa started coughing, and Silenus was suddenly booming out laughter. Jackson raised a hand, palm up, and flicked his fingers a couple of times.

"Come here," he murmured.

I raised my brows. Was he insane?

"Does anyone want another beer?" I asked loudly.

Not a single hand went up at first, but then two grinning men raised theirs.

Well, shit. That had backfired.

"There you go," I muttered as I put the two glasses in front of Jack and Rafael. "And you better tip me."

"We've come to an agreement," Rafael said.

What?

"I'd like to hear about this," Grandma Hazel chirped, and added, "In my role as the chaperone, of course."

"Chaperone?" Rafael asked.

"Don't ask," Jack muttered. "You'll find out soon enough."

"Agreement?" I snapped.

"Right," Jack said. "We both want to..." His eyes slid over to Grandma, and then back to me. "Take you on dates."

I was pretty sure those weren't the words they'd used when discussing me.

"So, we will," Rafael said.

What?

"No."

"Why not?" Grandma Hazel asked.

Since I had no suitable answer to give her, I ignored her and focused on why Rafael was there in the first place.

"You said you wanted me to find something?"

Jack sighed, but I ignored him too.

"My friend Gabe lost his purse, probably somewhere in Cathedral Park. He's got things in it that are of... sentimental value."

"Hasn't he looked for it himself?"

"Of course," Rafael said. "An old lady said that a dog grabbed it and ran off."

"I'm not a very good tracker," I told him.

"I'm a schuper duper tracksher," one of the triplets suddenly felt the need to share, and he did it in a decidedly slurry voice.

I turned to look at him.

"Are you drunk?" I asked slowly.

"Yup," he hiccupped with a happy grin.

"That's weird," I said, leaned over the bar and roared, "Because I've given you non-alcoholic beer all night, you underage twit!"

That sobered him up.

"What's the old lady's name?" I asked Rafael.

I got the details and glanced over on Joel to make

sure he caught everything too.

"I'll see what I can do," I murmured.

"Good," Rafael said, and Jackson murmured something which sounded suspiciously like the f-bomb.

"So, Kitty. Who's first?" Rafael said with a grin.

"First?"

"Dates," Jackson clarified. "And I'm first."

They were going to take turns?

"We're having a karaoke night at the community center on Wednesday," Grandpa Hunter shared. "It'll be a blast."

"You're first," Rafael quickly agreed with Jackson.

And there was the f-bomb again.

"Excellent," Grandpa said and rubbed his hands together. "You can even borrow my penis-enlarger if you need it," he offered Jackson.

There was a stunned moment of silence during which Jackson's face darkened, and I could tell that I would most likely have one grandfather less in a few seconds, so I prepared to intervene when the door was opened with considerable force.

A chubby man with short arms and a scowl on his face marched in.

"You ruined my life," he shouted, and I recognized him.

Last time I'd seen that troll, he'd been naked. And sitting on me.

Well, shit.

CHAPTER 10

Beetroot sherry

"How many times did you have to shower to get the mucus out?" Joel asked as he parked the car in the small parking lot next to the boat ramp.

"Three," I mumbled and let my gaze slide around Cathedral Park, not entirely sure what I was looking for.

The stupid purse wouldn't just come running out of the rhododendron bushes shouting my name. Or, it might, since it apparently had magical powers, but I hoped it wouldn't because that would seriously freak me out.

"He was so sad," Elsa said, and I saw her pale blue eyes glitter with friggin' tears.

I rolled my eyes and tried my best to say nothing at all about her misplaced sympathies because really? She was my friend, and I had been sat on by a troll again.

The troll had admittedly sobbed uncontrollably, but I got toll-goop in my hair, and most of the bar laughed at me, so she should really feel sorrier for me than the short-armed blubbering dude who only had himself to blame for his misery.

"He was," she insisted. "He really loves that woman, Kitty. We have to help him."

Uh, no.

"Where does the old lady live?" I asked Joel instead of getting into an argument with Elsa.

"Up there," Joel said and pointed up the hill. "Decateur Street."

I was out of breath when we rang the doorbell. Joel was panting too. Elsa smiled sweetly at us and whinnied softly. And smugly.

"Yes?" a small, old woman asked suspiciously.

Aha, I thought. A crony. Since cronies were regulars who were under the protection of wizards, it made sense that no one had been able to make her tell them what she'd seen. It also posed a wee problem for us since we wouldn't be able to either.

"Hello," I said. "I'm Kitty, and we're –"

"Company!" she squealed and disappeared into the house.

I blinked and turned to my friends who were blinking too. They looked stupid, which meant I probably did, so I nudged Joel, and we followed the woman into her home.

"Sit down," she said amicably, and we did.

"I'm Kitty, and —"

My second attempt at interacting with her was foiled by another squeal.

"Sherry!"

She reached into a cupboard to the side and brought out a crystal decanter and glasses. The content of the carafe was dark red.

It looked like blood.

"Uh," I wheezed, but then the smell hit my nostrils.

What the hell was that?

"Beetroot sherry," she explained happily. "I make it myself."

Oh, God.

***

Getting up to Mrs. Decateur — yes same name as the street she was living on — had been hard. Getting back down proved to be harder, and it did this because we were so highly inebriated we could not be described as anything other than shit-faced.

Or, "Shee-it-faced," as Joel giggled when we stumbled along the side of the road.

A six feet six widget, giggling like a five-year-old girl while he tried to adjust his red mohawk which was partially coming out of its rubber band wasn't attractive. It was funny, but not attractive.

"Sherry-sherry lady, going through emotion," Elsa sang.

Mrs. Decateur had made us listen to old hits from

the eighties, and she was apparently a huge fan of a German band called Modern Talking. There was not one modern thing about them, but I had to admit that after five glasses of beetroot sherry, their songs had been catchy.

"Pretty sure the lady is called Cheri," Joel said with a frown.

"Love is where you find it" Elsa belted out. *"Listen to your heaaaaaart!"*

I stopped and stared at her.

"Your mouth is purple," I shared.

She stopped singing and stretched the tip of her tongue out far enough to wiggle it in front of her eyes. It was about as attractive as Joel's giggle.

"Sure is," she agreed. "Oopsie."

Joel was about to say something when I felt a familiar warmth wash over me.

No.

No, no, no.

Not now. Not when I was drunk off my ass and had a purple mouth from drinking way too much beetroot homebrew.

"Hey, babe," Rafael said. "Any luck so far?"

"Not really," I said, although I did this with my mouth mostly closed, so it came out a bit garbled.

"Okay. Didn't think so," he said. "This is my buddy, Gabe."

My head swiveled around to look at the man who apparently felt it was okay to walk around with a leather manbag in a strap around his wrist.

He was tall, built, blonde and stunning. I tried to

picture him with a cognac-colored murse dangling from his hand. I couldn't do it.

"Hello," he said, eyeing me suspiciously.

"Hey," I mumbled, and added, "Sorry about your bag. We'll find it."

Since I didn't open my mouth, it came out as, "Shoy bo bag. Yill kindi."

His eyes widened, and he turned to Rafael who was staring at me.

"This is who you employed?"

"Hey," I snapped.

"You are drunk," Gabe stated, which was accurate.

I didn't like the condescending tone of his voice, though, so I put a hand in front of my mouth and glared at him.

"And you are a manbag-wearing moron," I retorted.

"Kitty," Rafael said.

It sounded as if he was trying not to laugh.

"Carrying the sacred rocks of Machaerus in my hands weren't exactly practical."

"I'm pretty sure the sacred rocks of Macarena would have been good in a plastic bag, preferably one from the Harley-store or Bass pro shop. Or else you could have used a backpack like a normal man."

"Machaerus. The fortress where John the bap –"

"Whatever."

We were glaring angrily at each other, although my upper body was teetering from side to side and I was pretty sure my eyes had crossed ever so slightly.

"Remove your hand," Gabe ordered.

"No."

His brows went up, and he turned with a hoarse hiss toward Rafael.

"You get it now?" Rafael asked with a smirk.

"Get what?" I snapped

"Kitty, please tell me why you have your hand over your mouth," Rafael said, and I closed my eyes.

"Nuh-huh," I murmured.

"Jesus," Joel muttered.

"What's our cousin doing here?" Gabe asked, sounding surprised.

I opened my eyes and stared into Rafael's now laughing ones.

"We've had lots of sherry," Elsa informed everyone. "Lots," she added as a clarification, but since she was swaying, it might not have been needed to add that particular piece of clarity.

"Beetroot," Joel said.

"Kitty?" Rafael asked, and I stuck the tip of my tongue out.

✳✳✳

I tried to sneak into the house without my father noticing the state of me, and it did not work. This was partly because I walked right into him, but mostly because Elsa was still singing Modern Talking. Loudly, although she had moved on to sing about her brother Louie, which was kind of funny since Joel's brother was called Louis, so I was also laughing just about as loudly as she was singing.

"Karaoke night!" Grandpa Hunter yelled from the kitchen. "Elsa, you have to come too!"

"Kitty?"

I stared up at my father and tried to keep my eyes from crossing.

"Uh-huh," I confirmed, in case he needed to know that the swaying, purple-mouthed individual in front of him was indeed his oldest daughter.

Dad was about to start scolding me when he noticed Rafael.

"Who are you?" he asked in a way I thought was rude.

Mostly because it was.

"Hello, Sir. I'm Rafael Moya, and I couldn't let your daughter and her friends drive themselves up here, so I took Kitty home in my car."

Wow. He sounded like a grown-up.

"Huh," Dad said, clearly unhappy about an unknown man visiting whilst looking like sex-on-legs and standing close to his daughter's back.

He was however quite aware that he should be grateful someone had taken care of us, and that if Rafael hadn't stood where he stood, I would have fallen over backward. The conflicting emotions passing over his face made him look like he needed to poop. Urgently.

"What are you?" Dad asked when the silence stretched out into embarrassing, not even trying to hide how he was sniffing the air.

"Half angel, half satyr," Rafael said calmly. "Kitty

works for my uncle."

My mouth fell open, which was unfortunate because Dad's angry gaze saw the effects of Mrs. Decateur's sherry and his eyes widened.

"What the hell have you done?"

"Um."

"Hello everyone!" a happy voice chirped.

Yes! Saved by my elders.

"Grandma!" I squealed.

"You've been to see Genie, I see," she said calmly.

"Genie?"

"Genie Decateur. We went to school together."

Of course they did.

"I dated her," Grandpa Hunter shared from the kitchen door. "Loony."

I wasn't sure if it was Mrs. Decateur, him or the date that had been loony, and since I suspected it could very well be all three, I decided not to ask. My head had also started pounding, and I wanted to lie down for a bit.

"We wanted to know about a bag that went missing in Cathedral Park," I said. "She wasn't talking."

"That's Genie," Grandma sighed. "I'll give her a call."

She surveyed my appearance, mumbled a few words and my eyes widened. I heard Joel and Elsa exhale.

"You can remove hangovers?" I breathed out.

"Didn't you even learn the useful stuff in witch class?" she snapped, pulled out her phone and walked off.

I hadn't, actually, but I realized that I probably should have. This skill would have come in handy upon many occasions in the past, something I wasn't going to share with my father. Then I remembered what Rafael had said.

"Silenus is your uncle?" I asked.

"My mother's older brother," he said, which would indeed make the man his uncle.

"He's fat," I told Rafael.

"Satyrs usually are," he said calmly. "Mom's been on a diet since Cheri Cheri Lady played regularly on the radio."

Oh, crap. They'd heard our wobbly descent down toward the parking lot.

"Angel?" Dad asked slowly. "Not making me happy. I know how the lot of you make girls do whatever you want." He scowled and crossed his arms over his broad chest. "Not happy at all," he added as if we hadn't heard him the first time which we had because his voice had been loud enough to be heard all over Nowhere.

"Kitty doesn't obey me."

There was complete silence on the porch, and then I started laughing. Smugly and with no little amount of glee.

"Can you guarantee that?" Dad asked and glared at him.

"If you want a guarantee, buy a toaster," Rafael muttered.

"What?" Dad boomed, and I knew why he did this

because I'd heard him say those exact words a million times.

My life was about to get complicated in a way I was not looking forward to.

"Sorry," Rafael said. "Movie quote. Didn't –"

"The Clint," Dad wheezed.

"Yeah," Rafael said, but added with a small grimace, "Clint Eastwood. The Rookie. Not his best movie, but –"

"What's his best move?"

My eyes were darting back and forth between them, and I tried desperately to think about something to say that would stop what I saw happening in front of me. It was like a snowball, rolling down a very steep hill getting bigger and scarier by the second, and unfortunately, my mind might not be drunk anymore, but it was blank

Please, I murmured to myself. Please, please, please don't say –

"Dirty Harry, of course."

Shit.

"Do you own a house?" Dad blurted out.

"Live in a condo, but I have a small shack by the beach."

Oh, God.

"You have a shack by the beach," Dad repeated.

"It's kind of funky and needs –"

I saw my father open his mouth when he realized that he had a fellow Clint Eastwood fan who also happened to be the owner of a fixer-upper, and one by the beach, in front of him. Since I knew what he was about to do, I stepped in close and growled, "If you yell, I will rip out your intestines and wrap them around your throat."

Joel and Elsa had laughed since our fourth glass of sherry and kept doing it. I heard one of my brothers snicker somewhere in the vicinity. After a stunned silence, also Rafael started laughing.

"We're wolves, son," Dad said coolly. "She isn't joking."

Rafael's laughter died a quick death.

"Dinner's ready," Janie called from the kitchen, and I knew she'd heard every word, so I knew what that meant.

Dad knew it too.

"Would you like to stay for dinner?" he asked Rafael.

"It would be my pleasure."

"Excellent," I said and got surprised looks from around the porch. "I'm off to work. See you all later."

Then I turned around and fled.

CHAPTER 11

Pookie

I was running as fast as possible.

This was in no way something I enjoyed doing, which meant I rarely did and hence struggled a little getting enough oxygen into my lungs.

We were chasing a dog, and not any old dog at all. Pookie.

Last time I'd seen the stupid animal, he'd just relieved himself all over my leg, after which I'd growled. He'd peed some more before he disappeared, although out of fear and not on me. Pookie had apparently been gone since then, and the distraught owner had tried to find him with limited success.

When Grandma showed up at Tiaso's with a wide grin, I knew she'd talked to Genie Decateur in person. I knew this because her mouth was purple, although the fact that she was shee-it-faced was another indication. She managed to convey what Mrs. Decateur had shared about the dog running off with the manbag, and it took me a while to realize that the danged culprit was my nemesis, Pookie. It took Joel a lot less time, and he hooted with glee.

Jackson had been in the bar, and he hadn't heard about why I had been forced to move back home, but Joel shared the story in a perfectly ridiculously embellished way. I thought Jack would never stop laughing, so I told him Rafael was having dinner with my parents.

That shut him up.

The rest of the shift was eerily calm, except for the minor scuffle when Grandma Hazel decided to try her dancing skills at the pole. One of the bikers puked, although that could have been due to the thirteen jaeger-shots he'd consumed in less than half an hour. Three biker-babes started cheering, and Silenus clapped his hands, which in no way helped me to get Grandma off the stage sooner rather than immediately. She pouted a bit, but I bribed her with a margarita containing absolutely no alcohol which settled her down until my shift was over. Jackson trailed Grandma and me home and helped me wrestle her into the guest house and into bed.

Grandpa Hunter waited for us on the porch, looking serious. At least, I think that's the look he aimed for. He'd pursed his mouth, lowered his brows and was shaking his head from side to side, snorting rhythmically. It looked exactly as ridiculous as it sounds.

"Pow-pow," he said and pointed at Jackson.

"What?" Jackson asked which I found eminently understandable.

"We need to have a small meeting, and I can't say the other word because it's disrespectful and offensive."

"Just like your goddamned swim trunks then," I snapped.

"Whatever. We need to talk, Jackson. You have angelic issues."

"I heard," Jackson said calmly. "I'm not too worried, Hunter. The dude's a douche."

"A douche who knows every line from every Clint Eastwood movie ever made and owns a fixer upper by the beach. One who gets up after dinner and does the dishes like a goddamned pussy, without anyone asking him to do it. And who plays ball after dinner with her brothers, and does it well but still lets them win."

By the sound of things, my family had enjoyed having Rafael over for dinner.

"Huh," Jackson said.

"I'm going to bed," I said and moved.

This move was stopped abruptly by Jack's firm hand on my upper arm.

"Guess my timeline changed," he murmured and pulled me closer.

I was acutely aware that my grandfather was less than three feet away, staring curiously at us.

"Wh —"

I wanted to ask what he meant but I couldn't.

The reason I couldn't was that his mouth was on mine and we were kissing. I could have labeled this as him kissing me, but that would have been a big fat lie, unfortunately. When his tongue slid into my mouth, I immediately experienced a minor leakage of brain cells and kissed him back. Enthusiastically.

"Wow," I breathed when he straightened.

"Go to bed Kitty," he murmured, turned me around and pushed me toward the door in a way that probably was supposed to be gentle but due to his wolf-genes mostly was a shove that made me stumble a little.

I had no clue what to say, so I said nothing at all and walked inside.

"Excellent," I heard Gramps say. "Now, about the karaoke-night. I have an idea…"

I did not want to know what crazy ideas he'd unleash on Jack, so I kept walking and didn't stop until I was face down on my bed.

Joel and Elsa picked me up the next morning, took one look at me and started laughing.

"What?" I asked sourly.

"Kitty and Jackson, sitting in a tree, k-i-s —"

"Shut up," I snarled. "How the hell did you know he kissed me last night?"

"Aura," Elsa said and waved her hand in a wide circle in front of me.

"He told me," Joel said.

I stared at him.

"Told you?" I echoed.

"Well, perhaps not me, exactly. He told his brother. In a chat."

Aha. Jackson really should have known better.

"What did he say?" I asked, and cringed because it was such a high schooley thing to ask.

"That he kissed you."

"That's all?"

"They moved on to discuss the rash Parker got on his balls after shaving them, and how it looked like something he got after visiting a bar in Hong Kong. Then they talked for a very, very long time about chasing rabbits. It all ended with a discussion about shitting after eating Mexican versus Indian food."

I closed my eyes and wondered if pouring bleach in my ears could erase what I'd just heard.

"Holy shit," Elsa whispered.

"Not really," Joel said with a grin. "More like diarrhea, if the Vik-Hansen boys are to be trusted."

"Let's go find Pookie," I said, trying my best to not think about any of the things Joel had shared.

I parked Grandma Hazel's pink monstrosity next to Joel's small car, stepped out and spotted Pookie immediately. He was ambling around with what could only be described as an incredibly smug doggy-grin all over his snout and raised a leg to pee happily on some bushes.

I took a step forward which made Pookie notice my presence, and he froze immediately. Then he fell crotch first into the bushes, and a high-pitched wail echoed over Cathedral Park.

Pookie clearly remembered me.

"Go left," I shouted to Joel. "Go right," I ordered Elsa and charged straight ahead myself.

Pookie was in better shape than me, and also clearly desperate to get away. I jumped over a bench, crashed through the rhododendron bushes, legs pumping and arms waving wildly. The damned dog took a right turn toward the river, and I followed. Joel was shouting something, I heard Elsa laughing hysterically, but my wolf part was kicking in, and all I could see was the small creature running away from me.

Chase him. I had to chase him. Hunt the tiny thing down and –

"Hello."

I growled.

"Are you jogging too?"

I glanced to the side and stumbled, but kept going. A man was running next to me. He was in a pair of rather tight tights and an equally tight tee. What the actual fu –

"You don't recognize me," the man said conversationally, although a little breathlessly.

"No," I panted and increased my arm movements as if this would make my speed increase, which it didn't.

"I've bought drinks from you at Tiaso's. I hang with the bears."

He smelled like a regular, and I assumed he meant The Bears MC, who were garden gnomes, and not actual bears. They'd had a vote on the name, and The

Gnomes MC had not won. Neither had The Goblins MC, and The Hobbits MC's was protected since the days of Mr. Tolkien, who had been friends with a lot of creatures and also incredibly foresighted in his trademark applications. At a loss, the garden gnomes had approached the grizzlies who charged them an annual fee and let them call themselves bears.

I did recognize the man vaguely when I looked at him again.

He looked like the ordinary dude he was, which meant he stood out in Tiaso's. His average brown hair was average length. He wasn't skinny but not overweight, not buff but clearly not a weakling. Plenty of tattoos on his arms but not on his neck or face. Sweet smile. Just a regular regular. He also tipped well and never puked on the floor or fondled the dancing girls against their wishes.

"I'm Kitty," I wheezed out.

"I know. Wouldn't have pegged you for a runner, though. Not with that butt."

He wasn't wrong, but still.

"What's wrong with my butt?" I asked, turning left to follow a yelping Pookie who went in a full arc around the base of St. John's bridge.

"Not one thing whatsoever, which is why I didn't think I'd find you here, jogging."

Oh.

"Thanks," I hissed and tried to increase my speed as we crashed through the rhododendrons again. "I'm chasing a dog," I shared and pointed at Pookie.

"Why don't you just call for it? It's a nice dog.

Been running around here for a while."

"Really?"

"Would have taken it home with me but we have two cats, and they don't like canines."

I could have told him that canines didn't like cats right back.

"Huh," I growled and tried to see where Pookie had disappeared.

"I think it sleeps over there."

The man pointed toward some bushes by the river, and I veered off immediately. I couldn't care less about Pookie, at all, and was rapidly approaching a severe bout of hypoxia, so when I reached the bushes, I fell to my knees.

Tiny stars twinkled in front of my eyes. My breakfast was about to appear for a second introduction. And I needed to pee.

"Hello."

Well, hell. My running companion had followed me in under the bushes, it seemed. He was nice, and he had pointed me to where Pookie apparently had made himself a home, but right then I didn't want to socialize with anyone. I grunted noncommittally and prepared to say something as soon as I caught my breath.

"If you die, can I have your body?"

What? That hadn't sounded like the runner at all.

I raised my head and stared at what looked like a homeless man. His hair was long and straggly, his brown clothes looked like they hadn't been washed in the last decade and he was missing one of his front teeth. My gut clenched immediately when our eyes met because the red glitter in his indicated with no uncertainty that this was, in fact, a ghoul. His high-pitched, hyena-like giggle confirmed his ghoulishness.

I moved backward slowly, hoping that moving would assure him that I was alive. Ghouls feasted on flesh from dead humans, or if they were in a pinch, on any kind of flesh as long as it was dead. I smiled, hoping that smiling flesh of the alive variety would be off-putting.

Then something caught my eye.

Next to the ghoul's skinny left hip was a square leather pouch. A wristband was attached to one corner, and the ghoul sat on it.

"Look!" I shouted and pointed at the river.

The ghoul didn't move.

"I'd rather look at you," he hissed. "Tasssty."

Or she hissed. It was actually not easy to tell the difference when it came to ghouls.

"I'm not dead," I squeaked.

"You will be."

Well, yeah. A couple of hundred years from now. Or seventy, at least.

"Move!" I shouted.

When the damned thing didn't do what I asked it, I shoved. Since he, or she, was skinny, he rolled right into the river. I grabbed the bag and turned toward the sounds of moving feet behind me.

"Found it," I called out to Joel and Elsa.

They grinned at me and slowed down but their

broad smiles suddenly froze, and they stared over my shoulder. I knew what was there because I smelled it, but I still looked. The ghoul was apparently unhappy with being shoved into the Willamette River. Water plastered the thin strands of hair to its gray cheeks, the clothes dripped muddy water on the ground, and then it opened its mouth to hiss out something unintelligible.

I screeched loudly, and both Joel and Elsa immediately added precisely as loud and hysterical screeches. Then we ran again, up toward the car this time. The bag thumped against my hip, and I heard a soft snorting sound I knew meant Elsa was preparing to change into a unicorn, which would take care of the ghoul but a big, white and glittering horse with a horn in her forehead would undoubtedly be somewhat hard to explain in case a regular saw us. Which they would. The ghoul chased us for a while, but its smell faded away, so I was pretty sure it had given up, and as we approached the cars, I slowed down and turned around.

Cathedral Park was empty except for an elderly lady who was walking a small pink poodle.

"Let's go to Tiaso's," I wheezed out, and reached for the handle to get into my car.

"Uh, Kitty, there's a minor thing you should know..."

"What?" I asked as I plopped my aching backside into the driver's seat.

The smell of dog urine filled my nostrils immediately.

"We found Pookie," Elsa said.
"Couldn't fit him into my car," Joel added.
Oh, crap. Literally.

CHAPTER 12
Karaoke-nightmare

"Gramps!"

My voice was both loud and desperate because I had no clue what one would wear on a karaoke-night at the community center in Nowhere. Polyester pant-suits would be my guess, but since I would rather be dead – and possibly eaten by a ghoul – than donning myself in one of those, I was at a loss.

"What?" he yelled back from the porch.

"Clothes?"

"Optional!"

Eek! Naked karaoke?

"Red tee and jeans or yoga pants and a flannel?" I squeaked.

"Tee and jeans!"

"Loose or tight jeans!?"

"Tight!"

Shit. The last had not been yelled by my grandfather.

Jackson Vik-Hansen had apparently arrived early.

I dressed in a bright red, tight crop top with a print announcing to the world that I was wild, and a pair of jeans. And no. Not the tight ones, but the low-slung loose ones which made my butt look pretty awesome. Jack might have spent more time discussing how he shat after Indian food than sharing every nuance of our kiss, but he'd still kissed me. With lots and lots of tongue.

When I reached for a pair of silver hoops to put in my ears, my gaze fell on the pile of cash on my nightstand, and since I knew my brothers well, I pushed it into a drawer and put a few of my silver bracelets on top. The triplets were a lot more werewolf than me so they couldn't move the silver. Ha.

I had all that cash for two reasons.

One; I returned Pookie and got the finder's fee. I tried to not accept it since I'd been the one who'd scared the stupid animal into befriending a ghoul and living the high life on the banks of Willamette River. His owner cried crocodile tears of joy, refused to take no for an answer, and pushed the money into my hands. Joel and Elsa got their share, but there was still a considerable sum for me.

Two; I returned the leather-murse to Gabe. He tried to get out of paying by ordering me to not request a reward. I stared at him for a while, and he sighed deeply. Rafael laughed and handed me another heap of cash. Three-way split ensued, and I added to my pile of rent money.

Gabe sighed again, and I grinned at him.

"Fugly bag, Gabe," I shared.

It wasn't ugly exactly, or at least not compared to other manbags I'd seen. It was clearly expensive, and the leather seemed to glow with a golden light.

"I like women who do what I tell them," he retorted.

I knew he did. Angels were pretty rare, but everyone knew about them, and especially girls who had fathers like mine. Rafael had said he was half satyr, though, and I'd had no clue what that was, but Elsa had explained about them being the followers of Bacchus. Everyone totally knew who Bacchus was, mostly because if there was a party and it was a great one; he'd likely organized it. He was apparently in rehab, but he was according to gossip scheduled for an appearance in one of the weight-losing reality shows in another month, so he was probably drying up according to plans.

Rafael was half of each but seemed to take after his father's side more, at least appearance wise. He would have looked a lot less hot with thinning hair and a potbelly.

"I wonder why Kitty doesn't obey you," Elsa said thoughtfully. "You are both angels, so she should. I'll investiga –"

"Arch."

"What?"

"I'm an archangel."

The way Gabe raised one brow when he announced this was snooty enough to rival my mother, although not on par with the Az.

"You can stay here and discuss lineage if you like, but I'm going home," I shared. "In Grandma's pink car which smells of dog urine."

"I'll take you home," Rafael murmured. "Someone will clean the car and drive it up to Nowhere tomorrow. Consider it a part of your fee."

"You can't kiss me."

He blinked.

"Just saying," I added and glared at Joel who was chatting with a cute and suitably slutty biker-babe, although still listening in on what I said so he was also laughing.

"I won't," Rafael said calmly. "Not before the second date. That was the agreement with Vik-Hansen."

They had agreed when —

"Okay," I said quickly before either of my friends could share that Jack apparently was sneaky like... a wolf.

We talked about the ghoul on our way back to Nowhere and he, or she, was apparently the reason Gabe had been there with the rocks in the first place. Ghouls had problems with sacred artifacts, and since St. Johns bridge was pretty danged special, they wanted to make him find alternative living accommodations. Rafael walked me to the door, pecked my cheek, and left with a grin at my brother

Tom who was watching us whilst snickering in a teenagery and hence moronic way.

I worked the day-shift the next day which sucked because bikers slept during the day. Or drove their bikes. Or whatever, but what they did not do was drink beer, so the tips were abysmal, and I hadn't been in a good mood when I went home to get ready for goddamned karaoke.

When I'd brushed my hair, I walked downstairs and out on the porch where Jack and Gramps were waiting. Elsa had bowed out, and Joel was not going to join me on what he said sounded like, "A date from hell." Jackson's brother Parker might be there later, though, and I looked forward to that. I hadn't seen him since he joined the navy several years earlier.

Gramps was dressed up in black suit pants, a paisley patterned, turquoise silk shirt with a yellow handkerchief in the pocket and an enormous, matching yellow bow-tie. It looked like he was wearing the enlarger-thingie again and it stretched the pants to the max.

Yikes.

***

"Tall and tan and young and lovely, the girl from Ipanema comes walking..." Gramps crooned, off-key and also a little off beat.

He added something that was a feeble imitation of a moonwalk, which made the crotch-enlarger slide to the side to settle on his hip, and I was pretty sure I'd die. Jackson was suddenly breathing hoarsely and choppily through clenched teeth, and I didn't dare to look at him.

The ladies attending the karaoke-nightmare at the community center cheered and wiggled their butts, likely thinking it would make them look either tall, young or lovely. It did neither, but it was not for lack of trying. The nurse from the old folks' home out by the creek was acting as emcee, and when the horror was over, she aimed her eyes at Jackson and me. Jack shook his head slowly. Mrs. Ratched turned to me, and I growled softly. She looked at Jack again and raised a brow.

"Later," he stalled, and added when she aimed a death-glare at him, "Want my brother to be here."

"Huh," Mrs. Ratched huffed, but then three women started punching buttons on the karaoke machine, and she got busy trying to assist with their song choices.

There was a small kerfuffle which the three women won, and then we watched in stunned silence how a group of ancient, skinny-wrinkly and white women belted out that it apparently was raining men. Next up was one of the speedo culprits from my parents' front porch who thankfully was fully clothed this time, and he did a surprisingly good rendition of Born to Run.

Melissa Moose walked in halfway through the song with a bunch of girlfriends, sat down and winked at Jackson, pretending she hadn't seen me.

Grandma Hazel breezed through the door shortly thereafter, accompanied by Genie Decateur, and they were both purple mouthed. Then Parker Vik-Hansen walked in, surveyed the gathering and started laughing.

He was still laughing when he hugged me, slapped Jack on his shoulder, and sat down. Then he laughed some more.

"You gonna sing?" he asked his brother with a smirk.

"I will if Kitty does," Jackson said with an identical smirk.

Aha. So, I'd be singing that evening, apparently, and post-haste too.

"Baby, baby, baby, oh..."

My head snapped around, and I watched with narrowed eyes how Loosey Moosey sauntered toward Jackson, ignoring everyone else. She made all the moves one would expect.

Shimmy down and up again; Check.

Wink in a ridiculously exaggerated way; Check.

Pout and wiggle her butt; Check.

Push her cleavage into his face; Check, although, at this stage, Parker burst out laughing so she lost her salaciousness and accidentally slapped Jackson on the cheek with one of her oversized knockers. Jackson shifted backward and closed his eyes, but I could see his black tee move at the waist, so I suspected he was laughing too.

When Melissa had walked back to the makeshift stage, hair-toss, and wink over her shoulder and all, I moved. Grandma Hazel cheered loudly, and the elderly crowd who all had watched me grow up chimed in. I hoped nobody would have a heart attack from my performance.

The piano intro was perky, so my audience started clapping their hands, and it took a while before the words I sang registered. My voice was clear and innocent, and I smiled sweetly while I skippy-danced happily over toward Melissa and her friends. Then the chorus hit her, and the audience with all the force I could put into my admittedly rather excellent voice.

"Fuck you. Fuck you very, very muuuch. 'Cause we hate what you do and we hate your whole crew so please don't stay in touch..."

Thank God for Lily Allen.

Within seconds the room erupted in cheers, and by the time I got to the second chorus, everyone sang along. I'd moved away from Melissa and was facing a large group of mostly old shifters who enthusiastically belted out the words fuck you with me. Unfortunately, it seemed that they had grievances to settle and they started pointing at the ones who over their long lives had done something offensive.

One woman leaned close to another to roar fuck you in her face, and spittle accompanied the message. That earned her a fist in her belly. Several others were screaming, and it all escalated into mayhem when one man tried to pull the hair of another and accidentally ripped off his postiche. Two other men were tumbling around on the floor, kicking Jackson's grandmother's wheelchair hard enough to push it straight into the cake table we hadn't even started on. She screamed and wiped at the frosting spread out over her face, Grandma Hazel was laughing hysterically, and Genie Decateur cheered but moved on to take a deep swig from a flask that I suspected contained beetroot sherry. One of Melissa's friends decided at that moment that she didn't like Loosey Moosey either and started poking her in the chest, singing along with me when I hit the chorus again. Jackson and Parker dove into the fray, trying to separate people but there were too many fights, and then Jackson was pushed into the sherry flask, so his hair got streaked with the pinkish-purple liquid.

I didn't know what to do, so I kept singing, and since the equipment seemed to have been set on repeat, I restarted when the song did.

Someone must have called the emergency number because right in the middle of repeat number three, my eyes met those of my father. He was standing in the door surveying the scene in front of me with a look on his face that could only be described as astonishment.

"Fuck you," I sang, although my voice wavered slightly when his brows went up.

Then he calmly walked over and pulled the plug. Silence ensued immediately, everyone froze, and after a stunned second their eyes turned to me.

"What?" I asked weakly.

Parker started laughing again, and after a while, Grandpa Hunter chuckled from his position underneath three other old dudes on the floor. The bald man looked at the wig he held in his hand and started laughing too.

"Never liked this one anyway," he snorted.

"You look better without it," Grandma Hazel said reassuringly, although she did it laughing so I wasn't sure she meant it.

He looked like an egg, so I was pretty sure she didn't, actually.

"Woo-boy, this frosting is fantastic," Jack's grandmother suddenly squealed, and I thanked the divine powers it was his happy grandmother who had decided to attend the evening, and not the one who already gave me the evil eye.

One after the other, everyone started laughing until the room was so filled with hilarity my father's words were mostly heard by me.

"Only you, Kitty," he sighed.

"It wasn't my fault," I protested.

"It never is, so why are you always in the middle of every shitstorm?"

"My genes?"

"Exactly!" Grandpa Hunter exclaimed. "Fantastic genes. Everyone knows that."

CHAPTER 13

Az goes biker

I choked on thin air when the Az walked into Tiaso's. To see my stepfather in my place of work was surprising on so many levels but the shortage of air passing into my lungs was mostly due to his wardrobe choices. He wore what everyone else was wearing in a biker bar, which was jeans, boots and a tee.

His boots were cowboy ones, and he'd forgotten to remove the price tag, so it dangled happily next to his left foot with every step, announcing that he'd bought them at fifty percent off. The jeans were a blue so dark I was pretty sure some of it would stain his underwear unless he was going commando, a thought that made me wince. I had for obvious reasons no desire to get any kind of mental image of the Az's balls, blue or not. His tee was pistachio green, and it had a ridiculous picture of a boy-band on it. I was pretty sure it belonged to one of my sisters because of the boy-band but also the cut. It was decidedly female which meant it formed unflattering creases around his non-existent bosom.

"What in the everloving fudge?" I murmured.

"Know him?" Silenus asked.

"Stepmoron.   Stepasshole.   Stepfather. Whatever."

Silenus started laughing in a way that almost made half the patrons fall off their chairs. One of the bears, a real one and not a gnome, accidentally filled his nostrils with beer and the snorting which ensued was not attractive.

The Az stumbled, and his eyes narrowed when he saw me. I smiled blandly, hopefully presenting him with the picture of perfect innocence. Then he strutted over to sit down next to the president of the Weesels MC, who were weasels, amazingly skilled at finding things, but alas; not very good at spelling.

"What can I get you?" I asked.

"A martini," the Az said. "Lightly shaken and then stirred, two olives and a bowl of peanuts."

"Jaeger," the biker president, Wee, grunted.

Yes. The thin, beady-eyed man was indeed Wee-the-weasel. His parents must either have figured it was a name he'd manage to spell, or they'd had a really warped sense of humor.

I handed Wee his shot and put a glass of beer in front of Az. His brows went up, and I shrugged.

"Biker-martini," I said, plopped a handful of olives into the glass, and moved down the bar to take an order from three dwarves, which would be a challenge as usual.

Silenus held his hand up as I passed him, likely hoping that I'd high-five him, which I didn't. I would have to crawl up and lean over the bar to hear what the dwarves ordered, and had begged Silenus to build a small stair for the shorter patrons such as dwarves, gnomes, brownies and such. He'd refused with the argument that me climbing like that while wearing a giant's hankie was more appreciated by his customers than the girls dancing at the pole on Saturdays.

The Az actually drank the beer, and when he was halfway through it, I walked back to wipe off the counter top in their vicinity. They were making a deal where the Weesels MC would hopefully find the missing amulet.

"I'd pay a million bucks to get that amulet back," Az sighed.

"I'll do it," I blurted out, surprising even myself with those words.

The Az stared at me, Wee grinned at me, and I heard friggin' Silenus giggle.

"You couldn't find an elephant even if you had it in front of you," Az declared decisively.

"But you'd give me a million bucks if I find the amulet?" I insisted.

"Unequivocally. Now go away," Az said and waved his hand dismissively in front of his face.

I murmured a quiet spell, and his waving hand slapped him on both his cheeks. I kept my innocent, bland face firmly in place and put a bowl of peanuts mixed with pickled onions and lemon slices in front of my stepfather.

"Kitty!"

I moved toward the old goof who'd called out and leaned in.

"Beer?"

"I heard you found Archangel Gabriel's manbag," he said, nodding which I assumed he wanted a beer, so I poured him one. "The damndest thing happened. I lost my wedding ring, and the missus has threatened to cut off my genitals if I don't find it again. I'll give you a hundred if you can locate it."

Yikes. The wife didn't have much tolerance for mistakes, apparently.

"Your genitals are worth a hundred?" I asked.

"I meant ten hundred," he muttered.

Huh.

The man who had been jogging next to me in Cathedral Park and kindly pointed me to Pookie's ghoulish home appeared next to the goof, and said happily, "He means a thousand."

I'd known that. Mostly.

"Okay," I said, not willing to get into my math-skill-deficiencies. "When did you wear it the last time?"

The goof looked uncomfortable and squirmed in a way which made the stool he was perched upon squeak alarmingly. I wondered how badly he would hurt himself if it shattered underneath him and if perhaps Silenus should consider upgrading his decor. Furniture made from reinforced steel seemed more appropriate, considering his clientele.

"I took it off in the parking lot outside a place where it didn't seem suitable to wear. Put it in my pocket." He paused, and I kept watching him. "Uh, it was outside this club called Pussy-Pussy-Pussy."

Aha. I could see why the wife would object in such a violent way to the ring being lost.

"I was only there to pick up a pal."

"Sure," I said, which seemed like an appropriate response to his blatant lie.

"We'll do it!" the jogging man said excitedly.

I turned and was about to protest when the goof's phone rang, so he tossed some bills on the bar and he walked away with a grin, calling out to us over his shoulder.

"Excellent, let me know when you've found it!"

The old man was so distracted by calling out to us and accepting the phone call that he almost walked straight into Joel and Elsa who apparently had decided to keep me company that evening. As expected, three biker-dudes got up and began moving chairs and people to clear the path for Elsa through a less than half full bar. She smiled sweetly, and one of them fainted. Joel stepped over the fat man and ushered Elsa forward. One of the biker-babes rubbed up against him, and her husband tried to hit Joel in the face, which he avoided with ease nimble enough to make it clear he was used to angry biker-husbands swiping at him.

I ignored the mayhem my friends caused and stared at the regular in front of me.

"We'll do it?" I drawled out.

"It's easy. The goof dropped it somewhere at that place, so we go there, find it, and collect the pastry."

My annoyance was swiftly replaced by confusion.

"Pastry?"

"He means the cake," Joel said as he sat down. "Cash," he clarified as if I was stupid.

I kept ignoring him.

"You," I said and pointed at the man, who reared back a little. "What's your name?"

He suddenly grinned happily again, and said chirpily, "I can call you Betty."

There was suddenly a chorus of low laughter on the other side of the bar, and I realized that his friends, the garden gnomes of the Bears MC, were with him. I really needed Silenus to build a platform or something.

"Huh," was the only thing I could think of saying, but in case he'd forgotten, I added slowly, "Except my name is Kitty."

"A man walks down the street, he says why am I soft in the middle?"

I blinked. The man was singing that question, and I wasn't sure if he wanted me to answer him. Since I didn't think he wanted to know that too many carbs were probably the answer, I blinked again and ignored the laughter from beneath the bar.

"Paul Simon?" the man said with a smile.

Yeah, I knew who Paul Simon was. Everyone did

which was partly because the man was one of the most gifted musicians of our times. Mostly it was because there was a persistent rumor that he was a warlock, of the Wicca variety. It had never been confirmed, but a man who released an album called 'Parsley, Sage, Rosemary, and Thyme' was not a regular, as far as I was concerned.

I still didn't get it.

The man kept singing, and when he got to the chorus, a surprisingly loud choir of voices from around the bar chimed in.

"... I can call you Betty, and Betty when you call me, you can call me Al."

You'd think someone who'd grown up in a virtual tsunami of dad-jokes should have gotten that one a lot sooner. The chuckles from around the bar told me that it wasn't the first time he'd pulled that stunt, but since it actually was mildly amusing, and since he was so obviously pleased with himself, I couldn't find it in me to get angry.

"You could have just told me," I sighed. "Al."

"I'll be your wingman in the quest for the lost wedding ring."

I ignored the slightly weird choice of word and shook my head slowly, aiming a glare at Joel who was suddenly laughing loudly.

"Co-pilot?"

Now Elsa was laughing too, but she did it whilst nodding vigorously.

"Assistant?" he tried. "Kitty, please. I don't mind my job. It's an okay job, but I install goddamned central vacuum systems. There's no going around the fact that no sucking in the world will ever be exciting."

"I disagree." Grandpa Hunter pushed Joel to the side, sat down on the stool and grinned at the man. "I've found that suck –"

"Eek!" I squealed and pointed to myself with both hands. "Innocent granddaughter here."

"Guess I gotta have a talk with Jackson again," Gramps muttered, which I ignored.

"Assistant," Al repeated, also ignoring my lecherous grandfather. "I'll do all the grunt work. Please, Kitty, I need a little excitement in my life."

He'd widened his eyes and tilted his head to the side.

Well, hell. He looked just like a dog, and not like the Pookie kind of dog. He looked like a goddamned golden retriever.

"Al," I said reluctantly. "You started this mess, so okay. You just got yourself a highly temporary second job."

"Yes!" he said in a voice that was a little too much a squeal for my taste.

What the hell had I just gotten myself into?

"The first task for you is to find out where that place is located," I declared.

"Which place?" Gramps asked.

"Some seedy place where the old goof lost his ring. It's called Pussy-puss –"

"Corner of Warburton and Seventh," Gramps cut me off calmly.

"How —" I stopped myself because asking a question you seriously didn't want to know the answer to was just plain stupid. "Never mind," I mumbled.

That didn't stop Grandpa Hunter.

"Told you about that already. Howl, Yowl and I went there to..." he paused and wiggled his bushy brows. "Check things out."

"Howl and Yowl?" I asked, pretty sure I knew who he was talking about but too bewildered to stop myself.

"Bo and Andy," he said.

The speedo clad, crotch-enhancing old farts who had been with him on my parents' porch had apparently been given new nick-names. Grandpa didn't hesitate to confirm this too.

"Figured we'd need stage names."

"Stage names?" Joel asked.

I frowned at him and bugged my eyes out in a way I hoped would communicate that he was in no way helping.

"For when we're..." Grandpa made a pause, and there was another ridiculous brow-wiggle, this time aimed at Joel. "Performing."

I closed my eyes and wondered if I could find another family somewhere. Preferably in the far east, or perhaps in the Amazon jungle. Swimming with piranhas seemed infinitely preferable to hearing about my grandfather's performances.

"That sounds like a good idea," Al said, and my eyes flew wide open.

He smiled sweetly, and innocently, at Gramps.

"Don't ask," I said but it came out as a wheezy cough, and he either didn't hear or else ignored my advice.

"What's your stage name?" he asked.

Grandpa Hunter beamed at Al, the patrons of Tiaso's, and what possibly was the entire universe as he stretched his arms out and straightened his back.

"The furminator," he declared proudly.

Oh my God.

CHAPTER 14

I love lesbians

Rafael held out a single, deep red rose, and I moved to let him walk inside. Dad wheezed out something which sounded like a chuckle from his position leaning into the fridge, searching for God knew what, and I watched in confused silence as Rafael said something to my brothers which made them grin at him in a way that was surprisingly unstupid. Rafael winked at Janie and handed her a small box.

"Honey-fudge," he murmured. "Thought you might —"

"If I leave Biff, will you marry me?" Janie blurted out, and Dad straightened so quickly I worried he'd give himself a hernia.

"Sure," Rafael chuckled, and Janie grinned at him. "Are you ready Kitty?"

I was indeed ready, or as ready as I'd ever be for my first date with Rafael. Why I'd agreed to this weird double dating, of sorts, I had no clue, but I had, and we were having dinner. Grandma Hazel would join us to act as chaperone, something Rafael had accepted without objections.

Neither Rafael nor Grandma was aware of the portion of the evening we would spend at Pussy-Pussy-Pussy, mostly because I hadn't told them about it. Time was running out, though, so we had to visit the place, and it had to be that very night.

I'd sent my new and very eager assistant to check the place out, and Al had returned to tell me that it was indeed where Grandpa Hunter had said it was, it was indeed a bordello, and he was indeed not entering the place.

"Love my woman. Pretty sure she loves me. Want to keep a status quo on that and crawling around on the floor of a bordello might make things awkward," he said and blushed.

I hadn't known a man's ears could get that red. The Easter bunny's ears were the closest I'd seen, but they were a more pinkish hue.

"Someone has to go," Elsa piped in and watched me with a small grin.

"Tonight," Joel chimed in and moved his hand away from his phone. "Their schedule says the cleaning crew comes in tomorrow morning."

"You can go," I said to Joel.

"I have a date."

"I have a date too," I snapped. "I can't take Rafael

to –"

Then I cut myself off and grinned.

Rafael would be the perfect companion to that place. There would be lots of women there and if they objected to us searching the place he could just order them to let me.

"Exactly," Elsa said. "Just pop in on your way to the restaurant. The ring is probably on the floor somewhere, or in a corner. Grab it and get out. Bada-bing."

I was pretty sure the bada-bing-factor would be more or less nonexistent, but since I didn't have a better plan, I nodded and said we'd go.

And now I was sitting in the passenger seat next to Rafael, glancing at my grandmother and trying to come up with a good way to share that we would go where we would go.

When I'd cleared my throat the third time, Grandma Hazel murmured something.

"We have to stop at a bordello on our way to the restaurant," I blurted out.

Damned witchy grandmother and her truth saying spells.

The car swayed slightly, and Rafael burst out laughing.

"Okay," he said. "You got a particular one in mind, or do I get to choose?"

I gave him the address, and he was still chuckling when we parked outside a two-story house painted in a dark red with pink trims. Above the door was a neon sign that blinked out the word pussy in bursts of three.

"Ooh," Grandma squealed. "I've never been to a place like this. I might learn something."

Both Rafael and I turned slowly to look at her.

"Hazel," Rafael said quietly. "You might want to stay in the car."

"In your dreams, buster," Grandma chirped and got out.

We did too, and the three of us trooped into the place.

It looked like a bar, except it was quite early in the evening still, so there were only scantily clad women lounging around. When they caught sight of Rafael, they surged forward in a tidal wave of hookery desire to make their living off someone looking like him, which I admittedly could understand.

"Looks like you could take your pick," Grandma Hazel said with a smirk.

"Guess so," Rafael murmured. "Step back, ladies," he added, and the gathering in front of us all took one step backward.

All except one girl.

"Step back," Rafael repeated.

The group did what he ordered them, except for the girl who didn't move.

"See!" I exclaimed. "I'm not the only one who won't follow your orders."

"Huh," Rafael grunted, walked up to face the girl and murmured, "You'll walk back to the bar."

She started laughing which showed off a pair of pretty impressive incisors. Or, yeah. They were fangs because she was a vampire.

"Won't work, angel," she whispered. "I'm a lesbian."

At first, her words didn't register as more than a weird way of announcing her sexual preferences, but then the force of what she'd said hit me.

"I am not in any way a lesbian," I barked out before either Rafael or Grandma could draw the conclusion that I was.

"Do you have a problem with lesbians?" the girl asked.

The happy look on her face had been replaced by one that was scary in a big way because she was a vampire, but she was also kind of butch, and the muscles on her arms were quite impressive.

"No," I squeaked. "I love lesbians."

"Really," she crooned and started moving toward me with a glint in her eyes I did not like.

The way her mood swung made me slightly nauseous, and I wasn't sure what to do.

"I love lesbians too," Grandma Hazel said happily. "Or," she added thoughtfully, "I think I do. I have never met one before."

Grandma was watching the vampire curiously. Rafael was laughing.

This was not good.

"What's your name," the girl murmured as she stopped in front of me.

"Kitty," I wheezed out.

"So, pretty-kitty... you love lesbians?"

I didn't. Or, to be honest, I didn't really care. Love

who you want was my view, so I hadn't thought much about which team anyone I met batted for. I took a deep breath and decided to get to why we were there instead of debating my feelings about homosexuality.

"I'm looking for a thing a friend of mine might accidentally have dropped when he visited this fine establishment a few days ago and if you just let me take a really quick look we'll leave like a wisp of gray smoke before you can say Saskatchewan or something equally long and difficult to pronounce which you can pick yourself while we pop upstairs, if we may?"

"Huh?"

"Thank you!" I squealed and smiled as happily as I could because I was also a little freaked out. "Saskatchewan," I added and moved toward the stairs.

Grandma Hazel followed me, but Rafael stayed with the women who by then looked like a group of... well, groupies.

We only had one room left to look in when heavy steps echoed in the hallway.

"I know you," a female voice said.

I turned and watched a short, stocky woman with arms that were a little too short for her bulk.

Oh, great. Another troll.

"Hey," I said with a smile. "I don't think we've met bef —"

"You destroyed my brother's life," she yelled and increased the pace with which she was approaching us.

I looked around frantically, hoping to find an escape route that hadn't been there a few seconds earlier. Grandma Hazel was moving behind me, and then the troll hit my gut. I went down immediately. The troll roared something, there was a crackling sound, and then the goddamned woman on top of me went limp.

"Grandma," I wheezed out.

"Hurry," Grandma Hazel urged. "I don't know how long a stun gun will keep her down. One more room and then we leave."

She'd come prepared, apparently.

There was no sight of the ring, and I was ready to give in when the troll burst through the door. She tackled me, and before I knew it, she was sitting on me.

"Charge, charge, charge," Grandma muttered, and I heard a frantic clicking but not the crackle from before.

"Can we talk about this?" I asked.

"No."

I tried to wiggle my way out from under her bulging behind when I noticed a glint of gold under the bed, right between the mattress and the slats. Slowly, I stretched an arm out, but I couldn't reach the ring.

"I can meet with your brother," I offered, and tried to slide closer to the bed. "See if I can help him."

"No."

Damned troll.

LENA NORTH

"A-ha!" Grandma yelled.

There was another crackle, and the stupid woman went limp again. I pushed her off me, rolled halfway under the bed to grab the ring, and then we were running down the stairs.

"We have to leave," I yelled and didn't wait to see if Rafael, Grandma or the troll was following.

The front door to the first, and hopefully last bordello I'd ever frequented was thrown open as we turned onto Seventh Street and I waved in a way I hoped was friendly at the lesbian, a group of happy women and a very angry troll.

"Excellent," I said and tried to adjust my clothes and hair at the same time as I wiped a glob of troll-mucus off my cheek before Rafael noticed it. "Dinner now or..."

I trailed off when my eyes met Rafael's.

"Shower," he drawled out. "My place."

"Fantastic," Grandma chirped. "I need to recharge my little thingamajig."

"You do that, Hazel, and I'll help Kitty clean up and get her into one of my tees," Rafael murmured.

He'd help me get into one of his –

Eek!

✳✳✳

"Rafael kissed me," I said and put the bowl of cookie dough down with a thud.

"Of course," Elsa murmured and leaned back with a groan. "I'm never drinking lemon juice again."

"Could have been the vodka," Joel grunted.

"This is true," Elsa conceded.

I murmured a few words and waved my hand to close the spell.

"Ho-ly-shee-it!" Joel exclaimed, wide-eyed and with a grin spreading on his face. "I knew there was a reason why we were friends, Hibiscus my witchy darling. Knew it. Knew —"

"Shut up," I muttered.

"Thank you," Elsa sighed.

They had apparently had a blast without me while I was out and about with my grandmother who kept stun-gunning trolls and Rafael who insisted on kissing me, which was the reason I'd waited two full hours before showing off my newfound skills in hangover removal.

"What should I do?"

"Learn more spells," Joel said.

"I'm such a slut," I groaned. "Perhaps there is an anti-slut spell."

"You're not *that* slutty," Elsa protested, which wasn't incredibly reassuring. "Was he good?"

"God, yes."

She grinned at me, and asked, "Better than Jackson?"

"I don't know," I squealed. "Different. He did this thing with his tongue where —"

"Oh, for the love of just about everything, Kitty," Joel barked out. "Don't. Just... don't."

"I need to focus on something else. Something that isn't the two morons and their ridiculous kisses and muscles and tongu –"

"Ah, ah, ah," Joel said loudly and put a palm in my face. "Don't wanna know."

"The amulet," Elsa said.

I stared at her, and as always, she'd applied reason to the problem at hand. I'd simply focus my energy on finding the Azdjakzian amulet. I wouldn't have time to go on dates. No time for kissing.

There was a soft buzz, and I glanced down on my phone. I had a message from Jackson.

"Aha," I said, and added haughtily. "I wish I could respond to Jackson, but I can't because I'm busy finding an amulet."

"Kind of rude to just ghost him, though," Elsa said.

She had a point, so I moved my thumbs over the screen.

<I've decided to devote my time to finding the Azdjakzian amulet so I will not have time to see you in the foreseeable future. Best Regards. Kitty.>

I thought that was a pretty mature message.

"Babe."

I jerked around and watched Jackson Vik-Hansen walk around the corner with his phone in his hand.

"What?"

"Unless you want to see your grandmother arrested for unlawful use of a stun gun, I suggest you make the time," he said with a grin.

"Buh."

I wish I could have come up with something brilliant.

Or even articulate.

"Exactly," he smirked. "Wednesday. My place. Second base."

What?

"Second what?!"

"Second date."

"No. You said second —"

His crooked grin went straight to my belly, and the explanation of what he'd said came to a screeching halt. I was pretty sure I was also both wide- and wild-eyed.

"Oopsie," he murmured and leaned down until his face was all I could see. "Freudian slip."

"Um."

"I'll grill. We'll have a few beers. Sit on the rickety porch for a while."

That actually sounded nice.

"Okay," I heard myself say breathily.

"Okay," he echoed. "Gotta go. There's been a break-in at the pharmacy and being the newbie, I get to interview the senior citizens who might have been in the vicinity."

He walked off, and I watched his backside as he did, telling myself that I didn't ogle his ass. Much.

Right. I could work at Tiaso's, date two men and look for an amulet at the same time, couldn't I?

CHAPTER 15

Happy B

I could not work in a biker bar, juggle two men and find an amulet at the same time. Not when I also had grandparents like mine.

Grandpa Hunter was the assigned chaperone to my porch and grill date with Jackson, which would have been fun since he usually was hilarious, albeit in a way that mostly made you feel you'd entered a somewhat dirty twilight zone.

Instead of being his usual self, Gramps sat down on the edge of the porch and spent the next hour staring into the forest. He mumbled things every now and then and alternated between counting something on his fingers, and sighing. Then Jackson asked him if he wanted grilled rib-eye and Grandpa Hunter said no.

He. Said. No.

A wolf saying no to rib-eye was a dying wolf, everyone knew that. They even used it instead of expensive blood tests over at the healthcare clinic.

We rushed over to him, and he explained calmly that he needed to cut back on the calories, and that he had eaten spinach accompanied by a bowl of grated carrots mixed with pieces of orange to ensure his iron levels were adequate. I had no clue why anyone would make the absolutely horrific decision to mix oranges into grated carrots, so I worried more than usual about Grandpa Hunter's sanity, which was saying something about my level of unease.

It took a while, but Jackson managed to convince Grandpa that he wasn't overweight, mostly because he wasn't, and once we'd gotten three hearty steaks into his system, he seemed to feel better. He was still mostly quiet through the rest of the evening, although that could be because he slept most of it, curled up on a blanket in a corner.

Jack and I were back on my parents' front porch, and I had explained to him that I didn't want to be kissed, something he ignored completely when Grandma Hazel walked out in a tight leather dress and fishnet stockings. She wobbled on her black platform shoes, and I closed my eyes, hoping that she'd be back in her usual flouncy, wide, hippie-dresses when I opened them again.

She wasn't, but she should have been because her skinny knees were not what they had been in her youth.

"I'm going to class!" she chirped happily. "Made friends with the girls at the triple-P and they'll teach me. Silenus says I'll make millions if I just learn a few basic moves."

Oh, God.

I deciphered that immediately. Grandma had somehow befriended the hookers at Pussy-Pussy-Pussy, they'd teach her to pole dance, and my goddamned boss had offered her a job.

"The troll-woman might not want you there," I tried, hoping to avoid the disaster I saw approaching like a freight train in the night.

"She's the one who will teach me," Grandma said.

Yish. Grandma Hazel with her skinny-wrinkly knees and elongated cleavage, getting undressed while humping a pole was not a sight I wanted to see. Since the troll was about as broad as she was tall and had a behind the size of Montana, I could easily picture the pole disappearing in her butt crack, never to be found again. It was not a sight I wanted to see either.

"But the stun gun?" I asked, desperately.

"She says it tickles. Bought one for herself."

Jackson's arm around me tightened, which plastered me even closer to his muscles, and I had been pretty darn close already before.

I felt his belly quiver, but his voice was completely calm when he asked, "Do you need a ride, Hazel?"

Had he just offered to drive my grandmother to a bordello, in a get-up that made her look like she worked there? Or, as if she'd worked there four hundred years ago, at least.

"I bet on you," she murmured. "Rafael's butt is cuter, and you really should rethink that ponytail because it makes you look silly. Still went with my gut and put a lot of money on you. Now I know why."

Without another word, she wobbled off toward her pink car, stumbled, but managed to open the door at the same time so when she fell, she landed in the driver's seat with a small, "Oomph."

"You bet on him?" I yelled. "Who else is in on the betting?"

She waved and closed the door. I tried to wrestle out of Jackson's grip and run after her, prepared to chase the car all the way down the mountain to get an answer from the old biddy. Unfortunately, he was a lot stronger, and also bigger than me, so all I managed to do was get myself picked off the ground. Then he sat down on the porch swing, placed me on his lap and went back to ignoring my request that he didn't kiss me.

"The douche-angel's ass is not cuter than mine," he mumbled between kisses.

"I like the ponytail," I said, mostly because I was pretty sure he wouldn't appreciate my thoughts about their backsides.

Jack had buns of steel, but Rafael's behind was a piece of art.

His head jerked back, and when his eyes narrowed, I put my hands behind his neck and pulled him down toward me.

"You should not kiss me again," I murmured.
And he did.

∗∗∗

I told Silenus I'd quit if he hired my grandmother as a pole dancer. He told me that if he didn't hire her, someone else would.

That shut me up.

Then he shared that she'd work one shift per week, and that shift would be Tuesdays between noon and noon-fifteen.

The simplistic brilliance of his plan was enough to make me grin, and then I went about my business selling beer and shots. Wee-the-weasel was there, and he just shrugged when I told him I was too busy and wouldn't go after the amulet. The goof stopped by and collected his wedding ring. I got the agreed wad of cash and tried unsuccessfully to split it with Joel and Elsa.

Al was nowhere to be seen which turned out to be since the Bears MC were on a road trip and had invited him to tag along. Why anyone would want to go on a road trip with a bunch of guys on kids sized dirt bikes, I did not know, but they were apparently down in Salem and wouldn't return until later. I put a third of the reward for the ring away and hoped Al would be good with the split.

I counted my savings when I got back home and realized that it would be a stretch, but I still had a chance of making the deposit for my apartment. An image of me on my couch eating cereal straight out of the box flashed in front of my eyes, and I fell asleep trying to figure out if it was nirvana or a nightmare I'd seen.

I slept like I usually did, which was deep and dreamless until a soft voice woke me up.

"Happy birthday to you, happy birthday to you…"

I stared straight into Jackson's laughing eyes. What the hell was he doing in my bedroom at that ungodly hour?

"Happy birthday, Kitty," he said and brushed his lips over my cheek.

I had forgotten my own birthday. Mom usually did, so Janie always compensated by celebrating me more than anyone else, but she hadn't said a word. I suddenly realized why Elsa had insisted we'd go out for dinner that evening, and why Silenus had changed the schedule so I'd be off. Jackson handed me a gift-wrapped present, and I smiled. He really could be so adorable, I thought.

He'd bought me a thong.

A bright red thong made out of lace and absolutely nothing else, and goddamn him, it was the right size too.

I held it up with both hands and wiggled it as I said sweetly, "I'll wear it tonight."

"What are –"

"Happy birthday to –"

My family stopped singing quite abruptly, which could have been because of Jackson sitting on my bed, but I suspected it was more related to the red garment I still held out for the world to see.

I tucked it under my pillow immediately.

"Chaperone!" Dad roared.

"I'm here," Grandpa shouted from the front porch, which was outside and also downstairs.

Dad took two steps and leaned out through the open window which Jack must have climbed in through.

"You can't be a goddamned chaperone down there."

"Okay," Gramps shouted back. "Coming up."

"Too late," Dad grumbled. "Happy birthday," he added sourly and threw a present at me.

It was heavy and hit me in the belly hard enough to push all the air out of my lungs.

"Biff," Janie said quietly. "Let's restart."

She walked out of the room, and the tone of her voice made it clear that arguments would not be appreciated.

Then they sang again, I opened my presents and answered texts from Joel, Elsa, and Silenus.

"Guess the angel forgot," Jackson smirked as he was ushered out of the room by my father.

"He's taking me out to dinner tonight," I smirked right back.

I did not tell Jack that Elsa and Joel had planned the evening, or that Rafael had invited himself without knowing it was my birthday.

"He's –"

"Guess I know what I'll wear," I added sweetly.

✳✳✳

It turned out that Rafael had figured out what the occasion was, and he brought a present too.

The small acorn was made of steel, and the intricate details were incredible. A sturdy ring was attached to its top.

"It's for when you get your place back," he said calmly and added, "Put your key on the ring."

Okay, that was nice. Useful, pretty, and sweet.

And boring.

"Thanks," I said chirpily.

"I know," he said. "Not sexy. But, Kitty. Get up and go to the restroom."

I blinked. How the hell had he known I needed to go?

A couple of steps away from the table, a soft voice murmured, *"You forgot me."*

I froze and turned slowly.

"What?"

"Keep walking," Rafael said.

Elsa and Joel were watching us with identical looks of confusion.

"Hey! Kitty, you forgot me."

I turned again, and again slowly.

"It talks to me."

"Yup. You won't ever lose your keys."

"You told him?" I asked Joel and Elsa.

They shook their heads.

"They didn't tell me anything," Rafael said. "But, Kitty? Someone like you is someone who loses her keys."

Yeah, okay. I totally was and had misplaced fourteen keys so far in my life, but I didn't want him to know that. Then a scent hit my nostrils, and I closed my eyes.

"Hibiscus?"

Double-shit. My mother, stepfather, and four sisters were standing behind me.

"Mother," I said, pasted a smile on my face and turned. "Hey."

"What are you doing here?" the Az asked.

"Having dinner?" I asked back.

"Fuchsia," Joel said, suddenly standing at my side. "Hello."

Elsa was there too, but then I heard my sisters' breaths become choppy, and knew Rafael had joined us. Introductions were made, although the way both my sisters and mother giggled when they shook hands with Rafael upset Az, so he snapped his fingers at a waitress, and demanded to be shown to their table.

The waitress pointed at the table we were standing next to and kept moving without a word. I couldn't blame her and wondered if I should snap my own fingers in the Az' face.

"Right," I said instead. "Well, you go ahead and have a nice dinner."

"Of course," the Az said, and turned his back to

me, but murmured over his shoulder, "We will not pay your bill."

"This place is expensive," Mom added. "Please make sure you check the prices before you ord —"

"Go away," Rafael cut in calmly, and she turned, walked around the table and sat down with a look of complete astonishment on her face.

"They forgot your birthday again," Elsa sighed.

"Doesn't matter," I said, which was a huge lie.

"Retribution," Joel said calmly and moved his fingertip away from his phone.

"What did you do?"

He just smirked, and then our food was brought in.

We'd finished our meal and was about to leave when I found out that I had the best friend in the whole world. I also had the craziest friend, which in reality was the same.

"Excuse me," the waitress said to the Az, and she was apparently still unhappy with him because she didn't keep her voice down much. "Do you have another card, Sir? The one you gave me seems to be blocked."

Five cards later, the Az was fuming.

Mom handed the waitress one of her cards, and five minutes later, the girl came back with a strange look on her face.

"Um, excuse me, Ma'am," she said. "There is a problem with your card too."

"It can't be blocked too," Mom said haughtily.

"No," the waitress said. "But the name printed on

the card doesn't match the one in the systems, so it won't go through in our machine."

"My name is Fuchsia de Chamontelette-Azdjakzian, which is the name on the card," Mom said rather loudly.

"Except..." the waitress said. "Your first name is spelled differently in the system."

"Differently?"

"The H seems to somehow have been replaced with a K."

My eyes slid to the side to watch Joel's carefully blank face, and I'd never loved him more than in that exact moment when I realized that he'd changed my mother's name to Fucksia.

CHAPTER 16

My pal, Al

For the first time in many years, my mother tried to visit Nowhere. The ravens told on her, so Janie was waiting in the middle of the road at the town limits. Mom chucked the fastest u-ey anyone in the area had ever seen, and the gossip-mill claimed that a cloud of gray smoke had been seen behind her car as she sped away. Janie had been partially in her bear shape, and I knew how menacing the pale, yellow glitter in a bear's eyes could be, so my mother's hasty retreat was in no way a surprise.

Joel had altered the spelling of my mother's name in more systems than the bank's, it seemed. He'd changed it in every single place in any computer system where my mother's name existed.

She'd consequently paid a widget-consultant a

shitload of money to sort it out. It would be changed back, but since the widget she'd hired happened to be Joel's half-brother Louis, it would take eight weeks until the correction was in effect. Until then, Fuchsia would have to spell out her name with the K everywhere and pretend she didn't notice how everyone – and I do mean everyone – was trying not to laugh at her. She'd arrived in Nowhere eager to yell at me, which wouldn't have helped, and probably to yell even more at Joel who was visiting my parents for a few days as a safety precaution.

Janie had baked a cake for Joel, and Dad had patted him so hard on his back he bumped into a wall and got a black eye.

Elsa was visiting too, which wasn't needed but she wanted to, and my father immediately said yes because he was even sillier than the biker-brethren when it came to her. When she glanced up at him and blinked slowly, he was immediately reduced to a smiling fool. This was a pretty ridiculous look for a werewolf, so Janie had laughed loudly while she put sheets in their second guestroom.

"I told you," Grandma squealed when we were gathered on the porch. "This is just like summer camp."

"With vodka," I added, and raised my glass in a silent toast.

My parents were attending a town hall meeting, Grandpa Hunter was participating in what he'd labeled, "A life or death Parcheesi tournament," and my brothers were helping Jackson install a new kitchen. The second Dad's truck disappeared up the road, Grandma had pulled out a bottle of vodka from under her deck chair and added liberal amounts to whatever we had in our glasses, and we'd been on the porch for a while, which meant that my observation was delivered with a slight slur in my voice. I was also feeling mellow.

"I love you. I really, really do, and I should have told you a long time ago," I said to Joel.

Elsa murmured a soft, "Awww," and Grandma echoed the sappy sound.

Joel's face softened for a second, but then he smiled his usual shiteater grin.

"I've saved that stunt for a long time, Kitty. Thought about it already back in high school but wanted to use it when it mattered. You matter."

He shrugged, and I squeezed his hand.

"Thank you."

"I hate them," Elsa said calmly and nodded when Grandma offered her more vodka. "I know you said you don't have time, but I really wish we could find that stupid amulet."

"Yes," Grandma said gleefully. "We could shove it up Aïdan's butthole."

I blinked.

"Or else we could just collect the million dollars he promised Kitty if she found it," Joel said calmly.

"That would work too," Grandma said, nodding sagely, albeit wobbly.

"Okay," I said against my better judgment. "Let's do it."

"I'll scan police records and see if there's something of use," Joel said.

"Yay," Elsa murmured. "I'll investigate whilst pretending that I'm working. Might keep me awake for once."

"I thought you liked the library."

"Liked," she agreed. "Past tense. It got boring, and I don't shush very well, so my boss hates me. Since the bikers started coming there, it's gotten more interesting, but it's still just like bad sex."

Huh?

"I've had plenty of that, and I still don't understand," Grandma Hazel shared.

Yikes. Way too much information.

"We hand out books, and people return books," Elsa said. "It's just in and out and nothing else. Like bad sex."

Ah. She did have a point.

"Hey," a deep voice said, and I turned slowly.

What was it with Jackson and showing up unannounced? Or showing up at all.

"Vodka?" Grandma asked and wiggled the bottle which was mostly empty.

"On call," Jack retorted with a grimace and a negative headshake. "What are you talking about?"

"Bad sex," Joel answered, and I kicked his shin.

My brothers laughed, as expected.

"Boys," Grandma murmured. "Bad sex is not something to laugh about. I've had it, so I know."

Ha. Their laughter turned into nervous giggles which faded away quickly.

"Jackson looks like someone who gives good sex. You should ask him for advice," Elsa told the triplets lazily, and drunkenly.

I kicked her too, mostly because I did not want to think about what kind of sex Jackson engaged in.

"I do," Jack said calmly. "Not sharing my secrets, though. Ask your dad."

"Stop," I yelled. "I can't have this conversation, so we're changing the topic right now. Let's talk about Grandpa Hunter instead. What's going on with him?"

No one knew, but it turned out that we all worried.

✳✳✳

"You're a wizard," Benny slurred.

"No," I protested. "I'm half which, though."

"Found my ex with a troll. Found a manbag for the snooty angel. Found a dog. Found Archie's ring with the hookers. You can find anything."

Huh. He had a point. For someone who was such an expert at losing shit, I'd been pretty ding-darned successful at locating all kinds of things lately.

"I need help," he said, and leaned forward, so I had to rear back in order to stay sober.

His divorce was final, and he'd celebrated for three days straight so his breath would easily intoxicate a small swarm of mosquitos.

"Okay," I said, poured him a cup of coffee and slammed it into the bar with a stern look.

"I can't locate..." He leaned forward until his torso

was resting fully on the counter. "My glasses."

I stared at him.

"They're on your head," I said and pointed to emphasize what I'd just said.

"Wizard!" he shouted and stretched his arms out as if he wanted to hug me which wasn't going to happen, and also made it look like he was trying to do the breaststroke over the bar.

Wee-the-weasel appeared from nowhere to take a firm hold of Benny's shirt and belt and haul him backward until he was back on his feet. The happy man wobbled off and started dancing on a completely empty dance floor, proving that white men should never try to wiggle their hips to any kind of music and definitely not to R&B.

"Jaeger," Wee grunted, and added, "Damned foxes."

I assumed he meant Benny, who was one, decided to ignore it and poured him a shot.

"I'm gonna look for the amulet after all," I said.

He'd been in the process of downing the shot, but my comment apparently surprised him because he missed his mouth by a couple of inches and splashed Jaegermeister over his face.

I handed him a pile of napkins and poured him another drink.

"Thanks," he said, watched me carefully as he tossed the disgusting liquor back and added, "You just go ahead and try to find it, darlin'."

Then he grinned, and it widened into a smile which became laughter when Al joined us.

"Good luck," Wee chuckled and joined his weasel-brethren at a table.

"I'm sorry," Al said contritely. "I didn't help as much as I could have with the ring gig."

The ring gig?

"We found it," I said, reached into my back pocket and handed him his share of the reward. "Your share."

He stared at the money and pushed it back over the counter toward me.

"No. I feel bad about how I handled it. Save this for yourself and let me in on the next thing instead."

"Nothing to feel bad about," I said, and went on to explain what had happened at Pussy-Pussy-Pussy.

He was grinning widely when I'd finished describing my grandmother's stun gun skills and told me that he would be my assistant for free if I let him tag along while I searched for whatever we were searching for next.

"It could mean visiting a bordello," I warned him.

"Yeah," he sighed happily. "I'm pretty sure my woman wouldn't like that, but if I explained in a way that made sure she never knew about it, she'd be fine with it."

It took me a second to get what he was saying, and then I grinned too.

"Your woman?" I asked.

He pulled out his phone and showed me a picture of an absolutely stunning lady. She clearly had Indian heritage, and her wavy dark hair looked like something out of a magazine. He flicked to another picture which showed the gorgeous woman with a teenager who had to be her daughter. She was super cute.

"Your kid?"

"Yeah. She has a father somewhere too, though."

Okay, I didn't get that and decided to not open that can of worms.

"What are we looking at?" Silenus asked.

Al showed him the picture, explained who it was, and Silenus stared in stunned silence at the screen.

"How in the hell did you manage to score with someone like her?" he asked which was a very, very relevant question.

Al was nice, and his cheerful optimism was growing on me, but he was a regular guy. This woman was not a regular woman.

"She likes my Oreo," Al said with a shrug.

Al had an Oreo? Just one, or a whole package? Or... please, God, I begged silently. Please don't let this be a euphemism for his private parts. I did not need to hear any kind of details about his penis.

There was a commotion by the door and judging from the oohs, aahs, and sighs, Joel and Elsa had just walked in.

"What are you looking at?" Joel asked.

"Al's woman," Silenus answered, nudged the phone around toward them, and when Joel's eyes widened, he clarified, "She likes his Oreo."

"Oreo?" Joel asked.

"You know," Al said. "Like, my Chaka Khan?"

Chaka Khan? The woman could sing the shit out

of anyone but what she had to do with Al was beyond me. It was beyond the others too, if the confusion on their faces was any indication, but then Elsa suddenly smirked.

"Does she do yoga?" she asked.

"All the time," Al said. "She's very bendy."

Then he blushed in a way I didn't want to delve into, but Elsa nodded.

"He means aura," Elsa explained. "And chakras."

"That's what I said," Al said.

It hadn't been, but I wasn't going to argue with him because I'd just realized how my assistant could be of actual assistance.

Al could go undercover and infiltrate Grandpa Hunter's band of brothers to figure out what the hell they were up to.

CHAPTER 17

Free pass

Al was gung-ho about going undercover. I knew this because he told me, and he told me using the actual phrase gung-ho, which was an indication that he was way more middle-aged than I hoped I'd ever become.

"You won't be disappointed," he said gravely. "I will go so deep undercover you won't recognize me. I'll develop a persona that matches theirs. Act like them."

Oh, God. Al in a speedo. Just... no.

"Okay," I said. "No need to go overboard. Just meet Gramps, ask him a few questions, that's all."

"Exactly. I'll infiltrate the brotherhood, gather evidence of their activities and report back asap."

Uh. I had created a monster, it seemed, but it was

too late to do anything about it because we had arrived at my parents' house in Nowhere.

Grandma Hazel sat on the porch swing and read a book.

"Yoo-hoo," she called out, threw the book over her shoulder and got up to greet us. "Who might this be?"

"A friend of mine," I said, and turned toward Al to add, "This is my grandmother."

"I'm Hazel," Grandma said. "I usually don't date middle-aged gentlemen, but I could make an exception for you. I like your tattoos."

"He's taken," I said quickly and pushed a suddenly reluctant Al forward.

"Of course," Grandma Hazel said. "What's your name?"

"I can call you Betty," Al said.

I rolled my eyes with a sigh.

Here we go again.

"Ooh, clever," Grandma said without missing a beat. "Come on Al, let's get you something to drink. Kitty's grandfather is inside, you'll like him, he's nuts."

I wasn't sure why the nutty part of Grandpa Hunter would appeal to a regular as regular as Al, but I didn't get a chance to question her judgment because Dad, Janie, and Grandpa walked through the door.

"Huh," Dad grunted and surveyed Al with lowered brows. "Who are you?"

Al swallowed.

"Hello," he said nervously when no one said anything. "I can call you Betty."

"Not if you want to live," Dad snorted, but Janie giggled.

"Funny," she said. "Hey, Al. I'm Janie, this is Biff and," she indicated gramps, "Hunter."

I bugged my eyes out at Dad, relishing the fact that someone had pulled a dad-joke on the king of dad-jokes, and he hadn't gotten it. This did not make my father happy.

"Which Clint Eastwood movie is your favorite?" he asked Al, trying to regain ground.

"None."

The silence was suddenly thick. Like, jello-thick and not in a happy jello-shot way. It was more an I'm gonna slit your gut wide open and feast on your intestines way.

"You don't like the Clint?" Dad asked menacingly.

I tried to pull Al backward in case Dad decided to maul him, but he held his ground.

"No, I don't."

Dad pushed out air with a wheezing sound that I'd never heard him make before.

"I knew I'd like you," Grandma Hazel squealed. "I don't like the Clint either."

Dad's head whipped around, and he glared at her.

"Hazel," he said warningly.

"Well, I don't. His movies are boring, and he isn't even sexy."

"Hazel," Janie said warningly.

"He isn't," Grandma insisted. "Do you think he's

sexy?"

Janie's mouth fell open, and her eyes flitted toward Dad and back to Grandma. Then she winced. Dad pushed out another hoarse sound.

"Janie?" he asked.

"Um."

I stared at the scene in front of me and wondered how the simple act of bringing Al to Nowhere could have brought this whole disaster on.

"Janie!" Dad repeated. "You said he'd be on your free pass."

Her what? Oh, God, my parents had free passes. They'd seriously discussed having sex with other people, and which ones they would be allowed to do it with.

"Well, I lied," Janie snapped. "Any sane woman of any age would put Brad Pitt on her free pass, and you should know that."

"Absolutely," Grandma Hazel agreed immediately and emphatically. "I'd totally do him. Wouldn't you, Kitty?"

"Well, yeah," I agreed reluctantly because really?

He might be a bit on the old side, but it was Brad Pitt. I was also pretty sure he was an elf.

"Huh," Al said. "He's on my woman's free pass too."

It seemed Mr. Pitt could keep himself busy for quite a while, should he feel so inclined.

"But," Dad wheezed. "The Clint."

"Get over it," I said. "He's old and wrinkly."

Dad closed his eyes, and I decided to use that to

my advantage, so I pushed Al in front of me, which propelled him into Grandpa who had to move backward. When we were inside, I closed the door, listened to the yelling outside, and grinned.

"Beer?"

Both men agreed that staying inside with a beer was eminently preferable to debating the sexual appeal of the Clint.

***

I sat with Grandma on a bench outside the garage and waited for Al. He had hit it off with my grandfather in a way I had not expected, and I wasn't even sure it was an act. They'd been to Bubba's. They sang a duet at the community center, and it hadn't even been karaoke night. They'd gone to places Al wouldn't tell me about. And now they were inside in the small apartment Grandpa had moved into, Howl and Yowl had joined them, and loud laughter echoed over the yard.

"How much did you bet on Jackson?" I asked and squinted against the bright afternoon sun.

"Plenty," she murmured sleepily.

"Who else is in on it?"

"Not saying."

Huh. Grandpa, probably. I wouldn't be at all surprised if Joel were involved. Maybe Silenus? I recognized the mutinous look on her face, though, and decided to change the topic.

"Can you scry again to see if you can find the

amulet? Joel searched the records, and the police know nothing about it even being gone. Elsa tried to read a few old scrolls, but the wizards got all hoity-toity about it and told her to give them back. I don't know what to do next."

"Sure," she agreed. "I've tried a few times, but I don't think Janie wants a bonfire in her backyard, so I've had to stop. We could perhaps try together?"

I wasn't sure adding me to the mix would improve anything.

"Perhaps Mom should be there too?"

Grandma turned her head slowly and looked at me with her brows raised.

"Maybe not," I sighed. "Okay, Grandma. Let's try to scry just the two of us. How bad can it go?"

I was pretty sure it could go extraordinarily bad, but if we pulled out the garden hose, we should be able to avoid a forest fire. I hoped.

"Not today. I need to prepare. Tomorrow I'm working my first shift at Tiaso's. The day after?" Grandma asked.

She was still blissfully unaware that her shift was fifteen minutes long so there would be plenty of time to scry in the afternoon, but I decided to let Silenus convey this.

"You really think you're ready to perform?" I asked, hoping against all odds that she would say that she wasn't.

"Mellie and Bellie both say I am," she answered.

"Who?"

"Melinda is the troll, and Belinda is your lesbian

vampire friend."

My lesbian vampire friend? Bellie?

I decided that a simple, "Okay," was all I needed to say since I would never again see either of the women.

Steps approached from the apartment, and I started gathering up my things. I'd promised to drop Al off at his place before going to Tiaso's.

"Yo!"

I closed my eyes and wondered if I could not open them again in a million years because Al saying yo in that voice could not mean good things. Grandma stated laughing and against my wishes, my eyes flew open.

"Yieee," I squealed and closed them again.

Al was right in front of me.

Let me rephrase that; Al's crotch was right in front of me. Al was probably ten feet away.

"What the hell?" I groaned.

"I know," Al said. "It feels a bit weird, but it looks kind of cool, doesn't it?"

It did not.

A car approached and keeping my eyes firmly on it, I watched as Rafael parked, got out and walked toward us.

"Hey," he called out.

"Huh," I wheezed.

"Hey," Al echoed and turned around.

Rafael took a double-step, and his brows went high on his forehead.

"Yikes," he muttered. "What have you got there,

Al?"

"A penis enlarger," Al explained. "Nifty. You tuck your willy inside and..." he trailed off and waved his hand in front of his crotch.

"Okay."

Rafael studiously avoided looking at me. I was mostly happy Al had turned his backside my way and was trying hard not to laugh.

"It's comfy," Al added. "It has some kind of soft fabric inside. Kitty's grandfather had it in a box upstairs."

Oh, God.

"Uh, Al?" He turned, and I winced. "You do realize that he's used it?" Al's eyes widened, and I added gently, "More than once."

For a second which felt like an eternity, our gazes held, but then Al's brain processed the fact that he had his private parts completely covered by soft fabric that had held my grandfather's private parts just as snugly on several occasions.

He screamed in panic and started pulling at his crotch. His jeans didn't allow for any adjustment of the enlarger, and he took a few steps to the side. With another desperate scream, he tore down his jeans and briefs, fell to his knees and then a beige item was flying through the air.

He was sobbing and wailing at the same time, and I wondered if pouring bleach in my eyes would erase the image of his white butt from my retina.

"Come on, man," I heard Rafael say quietly. "Pull your pants up. There you go. No need to button them." He put a hand on Al's shoulder and leaned in closer. "Go take a shower. Use plenty of soap. I'll make sure there's whiskey available when you return."

"A gallon?" Al whispered.

"A gallon," Rafael confirmed, gave him a gentle shove toward the main house, and added, "Hazel. Could you please direct our friend to the nearest bathroom?"

My grandmother was crazy, and often in a hilarious way, but she wasn't cruel. The look on Al's face was one of a man who would circumcise himself with his nails any second, and she didn't bat an eyelid.

"You can use my shower," she said softly. "I'll give you a couple of antiseptic wipes."

Al whimpered and followed her to the guest house.

Rafael sat down, turned and looked at me.

"Babe," he murmured. "Someone has got to get your grandfather under control."

"Working on it," I said hoarsely.

"Work faster."

There really wasn't anything else to say so we didn't say anything until Grandma Hazel had returned.

"Holy shit," she said. "Hilarious moment, but still... Poor man."

Rafael winced.

"Yeah," he said, and then he started laughing.

CHAPTER 18

Pimpleton

Ho-ly cow.

Grandma Hazel had been by the pole for less than five minutes, and she was already sliding off the thin shoulder straps holding her short dress up. If she kept this speed up, she'd be naked within two minutes.

"Do something," I wheezed.

Silenus didn't reply, so I turned and found him watching the performance with a wide grin. The incredibly drunk biker who was the only customer started clapping his hands. Since he was a fairy, his movements were oddly graceful, and the claps were mostly slow, soft whooshes of air.

"She's good," Silenus murmured.

"She's old," I snapped.

"I'm old too."

Oh, God. No. Just... no.

I leaned to the side and pulled the red handle which set off the fire alarm.

When the group of flabbergasted fire-fighters had left, Grandma's shift was over, and I had a week to figure out what to do next time.

"That was fun," Grandma Hazel squealed.

"You did good," Silenus murmured. "You didn't even seem nervous."

"I've practiced," Grandma said. "And as long as that disgusting wizard isn't watching, I like being on stage."

I only knew one wizard, and he was admittedly disgusting, but surely the Az hadn't been to Pussy-Pussy-Pussy to watch his mother-in-law practice her pole-dancing skills?

"Who?" I asked gingerly.

"I don't know who it is. He's stayed in the back, but the mood changes when he arrives. The girls don't like him and call him Pimpleton."

Pimpleton? That didn't sound like a wizard's name.

"Is he a customer?"

"No, that's the thing. The wizard says he's protecting them, and in exchange, they have to give him a percentage of... sales. The girls don't know what he protects them from, but he's powerful, and they can't say no."

Ah. The pimp part of Pimpleton made sense suddenly.

"Not nice," I murmured. "Are wizards allowed to do that kind of thing?"

"Nope."

Grandma took out an energy bar and started munching happily.

"Shouldn't we do something?"

"Like what?" she asked curiously.

"Like finding out who it is? If we can prove what he's doing, I can talk to the Grand Wizard."

I had no clue who the Grand Wizard was and suspected it might be my stepfather which would make the conversation uncomfortable. Maybe I'd be a wuss and bring my father along?

"We can do that," she said slowly. "When are you off?"

"I can handle the bar," Silenus cut in. "Don't like that shit, so you go and sort it out, Kitty."

Before I could stop to think about the wisdom of going to a place where a troll had sat on me, and a lesbian had... I didn't know what she'd done actually, but it was daytime, and she was a vampire, so she would likely not be there.

✳✳✳

As expected, the vampire wasn't there, but the troll was. She glared at me, which I ignored, and let Grandma Hazel do the talking. The girls were squealing happily when she explained our plan which wasn't a plan at all. It was a sketchy idea.

"I'm not sure I trust you," the troll muttered,

clearly aiming that comment at me.

"Kitty," Grandma snapped. "Tell Mellie about her brother."

In a few sentences, I explained about Benny, the divorce, the adultery and my part in it all. The troll winced when she heard how her brother had been running around the city in his birthday suit.

Then Grandma aimed her gaze at the troll, and said, "Do you have anything to add, Mellie?"

"He loves her."

I blinked.

"Mellie," Grandma repeated patiently.

"I don't have anything else to say. And she's a fox."

The divorcee was indeed a fox shifter, although I couldn't see the relevance of that statement.

"They'd have adorable kids."

Troll-foxes? I didn't think it sounded adorable at all, but whatever.

"He's clearly an idiot, but he loves her, she won't talk to him, and he doesn't know what to do," the troll whined.

"Kitty could talk to her," Grandma Hazel offered happily.

What? No. I could not talk to –

A phone was put in my hand and while the signals went through I tried frantically to think about what to say. Then a woman answered, I explained who I was, and she started crying. I stared desperately at my grandmother who was waving her hand in a way I had no clue what it meant. Then it hit me. Love songs made everyone happy, didn't they?

"What do you want to talk about?" the woman asked tearfully.

"The power of love," I blurted out.

"But I thought I wanted security. The money from Benny would give me that."

"Love is all you need," I said reassuringly.

"I don't know... I keep wondering, what's the meaning of it all?

"The glory of love," I stated.

"What if he's found someone else already?"

"You're still the one," I shared.

"But I'm a fox, we're an unusual couple, and –"

"A groovy kind of love," I said, nodding sagely, which she wouldn't see.

"Do you think he still loves me?" she said with hope in her voice.

"He's stuck on you."

"I'll love him forever," she sobbed.

"And he'll keep on loving you," I assured her.

"It's been so awful..."

"You are not alone."

"You're right. I will call him," she murmured.

"Perfect," I sighed.

"I'm not sure it's perfect exactly," she protested.

"Love can be," I said.

She sighed, but when she didn't say anything, I murmured a goodbye, closed the call and handed the phone back to Mellie. The room was completely silent, and everyone stared at me.

"What?" I asked.

"Magic," someone breathed out.

"I haven't heard that many cheesy song titles since that sappy valkyrie got married," someone else murmured.

"It worked, didn't it?" I said dismissively, although with a small smirk.

I felt pretty danged good about myself.

"He's coming," a girl who looked like a fairy but smelled like a puma suddenly murmured. She sniffed the air and nodded. "Pimpleton."

"He can't see us," I squealed.

We were shuffled through a room with a disturbing number of whips hanging on the wall, and out through the back door. A car was parked outside, and a man sat in the driver's seat, talking on the phone. Grandma and I squatted behind a dumpster, but when we heard him open the door, we peeked around the corner. His voice was a soft murmur, but I couldn't see anything.

"Get up," Grandma said and pointed to the top of the dumpster. "Hurry."

I jumped, and in my desperation, I used a little too much force, so I went too high up in the air, and on my way down, it became clear to me that there wasn't anything covering the top of the stupid thing.

As I descended toward the bags of trash, I saw the wizard.

His hair was colored in a way I suspected was meant to be golden, but it wasn't. It looked almost orange. It was also swept across his forehead in a strange attempt at a combover, which mostly looked funky.

He reared back in surprise when he saw me flying through the air, and our eyes met.

"Hiya!" I squeaked and waved happily.

He raised a hand, and as I landed in a pile of garbage, I heard a confused, "Hello?"

Grandma Hazel pulled me out via the side door, and we ran for her car. She laughed all the way back to Nowhere. I was busy removing pieces of God knows what from all over myself and did not laugh at all.

"No one will be at home," Grandma pressed out between loud bursts of completely unnecessary amusement. "It's afternoon, so no one will see you covered in –"

She stopped speaking abruptly, and my head snapped up to see what she was looking at.

There was a crowd in front of my parents' house.

Biff Brown, Janie Cameron-Brown, Bill, Joe, and Tom Brown, and Hunter Brown.

Joel and Elsa.

Jackson Vik-Hansen.

And Rafael Moya.

What the hell was everyone doing there in the middle of the goddamned afternoon?

I stepped out of the car, determined to act as if nothing was out of the ordinary.

"Babe," Jackson said when no one else said a single word. "Is there a reason you have a condom hanging in your hair?"

✳✳✳

It took more than an hour to clean me up, mostly because my father emphasized the need for extensive scrubbing with something antiseptic. Grandma Hazel promptly informed him that she'd used her last antiseptic wipes to clean up Al's crotch, and when Dad had picked his jaw off the ground, he walked away without another word. Janie refused to let me step inside wearing my clothes, so while everyone else was laughing, I stripped down to my underwear.

Then Dad walked back outside, roared hoarsely when he saw the red thong and poured a bottle of whiskey over my head. It got in my eyes, so I howled. He poured another bottle over me, and I heard another round of laughter.

"Can I lick it off?" Rafael murmured as he started wiping my face with his t-shirt.

Dad growled, but Rafael turned and looked at him.

"Biff," he said patiently. "Thong. Can you blame me?" Dad growled again, but his heart wasn't in it, so I guess he didn't blame Rafael.

"Looks hot, doesn't it," Jackson said calmly. "I got her that one."

Then he put his hands on my hips and steered us

toward the door. The whole situation was bizarre, but since I'd been idiotic enough to wear the stupid thong, I was happy Jackson walked behind me. I was pretty sure flashing my butt cheeks would give my father an actual stroke.

Everyone was waiting for me on the porch when I exited. I'd used a whole bottle of soap to wash off the whiskey and whatever else that had been stuck to my body, so I smelled like a goddamned rose garden.

"What was I supposed to do?" I asked, which I thought was very reasonable. "And what are you all doing here?"

"Your mother called," Dad said. "Said you started working at Puss —" He cut himself off when Janie kicked him and tilted her head toward my brothers. "Janie they're old enough to —" She kicked him again, and harder this time. Dad winced turned toward me. "Fuchsia called and said that you had gotten a job that was, uh, inappropriate."

I promptly told him and everyone else what we'd found out.

"I don't know who that idiot wizard is, but he looked like the kind of man who grabs your butt and pretends it was an accident," I finished my recount of the happenings.

"Malachï," Grandma Hazel said immediately. "Funky, fat, orange hair?"

"Yes," I confirmed. "Who is he?"

"He's the gatekeeper," Grandma murmured. "Guards the entrance to the wizards' headquarters, and their vaults."

"Another stupid spelling?" I asked since Grandma had pronounced his name Malach-ee instead of Malach-ay.

"They have an I, they do that shit," Grandma Hazel murmured. "They all want to be like Blaïse."

Bla-eese?

"Grand Master," Grandma said when mouths opened all over the porch. "His father was the actual inventor of the diaeresis mark, and woo-boy was that old goat a double-prick."

Aha.

"Excellent," I said. "Joel? Can you see if you can find out what this Malachï is up to, and then we talk to the wizards."

"Sure," Joel said and put his hand in his pocket which I hoped meant his phone was there and not that he felt like fondling himself.

"I thought it was the Az who was Grand Master," I said while we waited.

"Nope," Grandma said. "Aïdan is an Azdjakzian, and his family has yielded the power over the Azdjakzian-amulet for centuries."

"So that's why he wants to find it," I murmured.

"Probably. Aïdan has no real power of his own, so without the amulet, the Azdjakzians would be lower level wizards."

"Asshole," Joel suddenly exclaimed.

I could agree with that.

"This Malachï person is a naughty boy," Joel added sourly. "Collects cash from at least fifteen hor

—" He cut himself off with a glance at Janie, and wisely amended his statement. "Fifteen places of business all over the northwest."

"Well, crap," Grandma Hazel, muttered. "Genie will not be happy."

"Genie?" I asked as if I didn't know who the woman with the lethal beetroot homebrew was.

"She's a crony. Protected by a wizard. Malachï is the wizard who protects her."

"Poor woman," Elsa murmured and added. "No wonder she makes sherry from anything she can get her hands on."

"Okay," I sighed. "We'll just go talk to this Blaeeze-dude. Who's coming with me?"

Hands went up all over the porch.

CHAPTER 19

Artificial happiness

I'd been ready to go straight to the Grand Wiz and give him a piece of my mind. Grandma Hazel had been right there with me. Joel and Elsa had jumped in the backseat of the pink car, and one of my brothers crawled into the trunk.

Dad and Jackson placed themselves in front of us and wouldn't move even when I hit the gas pedal all the way to the floor. Dirt and gravel spewed behind the car and up on the porch which made Janie growl, something no one heard because of the rumble from Grandma Hazel's old monster of a vehicle and the roars from the seriously pissed off wolves who had placed their hands on the hood to hold us in place.

I jumped out of the car, and for the first time in my life, I wished I could shift into a wolf. I wished this mostly because when I jumped out of said car, Jackson changed and oh, my, God, he was gorgeous. A huge, gray timber wolf suddenly stood in front of me, baring his teeth and growling softly. All I could think of was running off into the woods with him and never come back to civilization again. Unless someone lured me back with a batch of cookie dough.

"Okay," Rafael said calmly. "Why don't everyone just calm –"

Snapping, sharp teeth missed him with two inches, and then an incredibly angry angel charged at the timber wolf. I was pretty sure one of them would get himself killed, although I wasn't sure which one, and was about to jump into the fray when a loud, shrieking whinny and the thumps of heavy hooves echoed.

Everyone froze.

Elsa had changed too, apparently.

The big, white unicorn moved restlessly around the yard, snorting and stomping. When no one moved, she raised her head proudly and glared at the crowd. Her tail made a wide, graceful sweep and then she farted loudly, spreading glitter and unicorn-dust all over the flower beds. A soothing scent of grapefruit washed over us with the soft breeze.

Everyone promptly did what everyone always did when inhaling unicorn fart; Calmed down and smiled gently. Elsa whinnied again and changed back.

"You can get up now," she said, and since there was laughter in her voice, I looked at what she looked at.

Jackson had changed back too, and Rafael was on top of him, holding a strong arm around his neck in a way that looked weirdly amorous. I was pretty sure it wasn't, though, and the subsequent man-squeal confirmed my suspicion. They got up on their feet so fast it was a blur and glared at each other.

"Kitty," Dad barked. "Porch. Now."

Okay. That was the dad-voice of all dad-voices, and I decided that it would be in my best interest to obey, so I walked up on the porch, sat down and watched the crowd in front of me.

"What?" I asked breezily because this time, it had so not been my fault.

Dad disagreed.

Then he explained in great detail how accusing a wizard of anything without actually having proof of the misdemeanor would get me killed, something which he at that stage informed me sounded like it wouldn't be too bad. Jackson made a scoffing sound and was promptly ordered to visit the bordellos in question to obtain witness statements. Joel didn't stop his laughter in time and was ordered to accompany Jack on his visits. Rafael smiled smugly and was told that his job was to keep me out of trouble until the statements were filed correctly, and if anything happened to me, then my father had no objections to filling a pie with stew made from angel-kidneys. He added that he would decorate this culinary masterpiece with angel-eyeballs or any kind of angel-balls at his disposal.

Rafael winced.

"Dad," I whispered.

"What?" he snarled.

"You've never baked a pie in your life," I informed him.

He opened his mouth but closed it with a snap.

Then he walked away without another word, and I stared at his back.

"That didn't go down very well," I murmured.

"Oh, I don't know," Grandma Hazel said breezily. "I'm pretty sure the throttle-thingie in my car hasn't been stress-tested that way before. Janie got her flowerbeds fertilized, which they needed. And we got to see Jackson and Rafael in a man-hug." She grinned at me, winked, and added, "All in all, not too bad?"

***

"My peanut is gone."

I wasn't sure if I was supposed to respond to that, but since the woman in front of me was an excellent tipper, and also a wolf, I decided to make an effort.

"Okay," I said, which was as much effort I figured a peanut warranted.

"Word on the street is that you're good at finding things, and I would reward you."

"Okay," I repeated, but the word reward did catch my attention.

The deadline for my condo down payment was looming, and I was still short of funds.

"I opened the window for five seconds and whoops. Gone."

I had already figured out that peanut wasn't a literal peanut, and wondered what kind of animal he, or she, was.

"And Peanut is your... dog?" I guessed.

The woman was a part of my father's pack, and canines were the prevailing type of pet in that group, mostly since any other pet tended to end up on the grill sooner rather than never.

"Lovebird."

I blinked.

"Lovebird," I echoed.

"Agapornis. It's a parrot. Small, mostly green with orangey marks," Joel murmured.

"Peanut is turquoise. His face is black."

"Huh," I said.

"He's from Namibia," the woman said as if this was an explanation of the coloring of her bird.

It might very well be, but since I was in no way an ornithologist, I had no clue.

"I'm not good with birds," I said. "Wouldn't know where to look."

"He likes peanuts," the woman said, and added, "And olives. Chips, unless they're onion-flavored."

The parrot liked bar-snacks, it seemed.

"But —"

"Just keep your eyes open. He'll come if you hold out some peanuts and whistle Oh Susanna."

I was about to decline but was sidetracked when Al walked in, followed by Jackson. The woman murmured her thanks, and I nodded absentmindedly.

"What's up?" I asked Al.

"I want to go over cover."

"Huh?"

"I've been under cover. Can't do it anymore. Not after the, uh, incident. I had to explain to my woman why my... *thing* is red. She did not like that I had to use antiseptic wipes on it."

Is red? Was it still —

God. I shook my head to stop my brain from delving further into that disgusting topic and nodded instead.

"Okay, sure," I said casually, and Al sighed with relief. "Do you know what they're up to?"

"Can't tell you."

"Can't tell me what?" I asked.

"They're —"

Al blushed so furiously I thought a vein in his temple would pop.

"What?"

"Can't —"

"Can you tell me?" Jackson interrupted calmly.

With a curt not, Al walked over to a corner at the other end of the bar. They sat down and stayed there for fifteen minutes and twelve seconds. I counted. Jackson barked out laughter sixteen times while Al talked. I counted that too.

Al left without looking at me, and Jackson walked back to the bar with a strange look on his face.

"When's your next break, babe?"

"When Rafael gets here," Silenus answered sourly.

I turned slowly, but he was watching Jackson with a blank face. Jack raised his upper lip and showed his teeth, which was meant to intimidate, but since he had a piece of broccoli stuck there, it mostly looked ridiculous.

"Boy," Silenus grunted. "I'm older than dirt, and a young whippersnapper with veggies in his teeth will not frighten me in any way."

I was pretty sure this was the first time anyone had called Jack a whippersnapper. I was also not sure what the word meant precisely, but it did not sound like a compliment.

Jackson did not take it as one, and the rumble in his chest increased in strength.

"Oh, for schmuck's sake, Jack," I snapped. "Go brush your teeth."

He turned toward me, and the rumble was still there, but he'd lowered his lip. I could see his tongue move over his front teeth, likely to remove the offensive and highly surprising piece of vegetable. In an attempt to avoid satyr-blood being sprayed all over the bar, I tried to make light of the whole situation.

"Shoo," I said breezily and waved my hand dismissively.

That had not been the right approach, it seemed, although Joel barked out laughter.

"Hibiscus," Jackson said sternly.

What in the everloving fudge?

"Yes, Mother, dear?" I chirped in a voice dripping with syrupy sarcasm.

At least, I hoped it did, but Joel was still laughing which made me suspect that it sounded mostly silly.

The stare-down went on for a while but then a familiar warmth washed over us, and Silenus exhaled.

"Boy," he murmured. "Keep telling you to step up your game. You're late."

"I'm early," Rafael retorted. "What's going on?"

No one answered, so he repeated his question a few times, to no avail.

Joel caved in first and explained what had happened.

"Broccoli?" Rafael snorted. "Seriously?"

"Or spinach," Joel confirmed. "Something green."

I kept staring at Jackson, not willing to give in.

"Kitty," he murmured softly, and the harshness suddenly left both his voice and face to be replaced by humor. "Would you please get outside so I can explain?"

"Of course," I said calmly.

"Not sure if you inherited that glare from your father or mother," Jack said and closed the back door, glancing sourly at Rafael who had exited the place with us.

"Spill," I said.

"Right. Okay. So, here's the thing. Apparently one of the girls, or possibly several of the girls helping the elderly in Nowhere told your grandfather that they wanted to, uh... procreate. With him. Told him he was genetically superior."

I blinked.

"Yeah, babe," Jack went on with a grin. "Hunter is under the distinct impression that someone wants to have his child. His friends, currently known as Howl and Yowl, got on board and they started a club."

"A club," I echoed slowly.

"Yeah," Jackson was suddenly trying to hold back laughter, failed at it and grinned. "They call it White Supremacy."

I blinked. And gasped. And blinked again. And gasped again. And —

"What the hell?" Rafael muttered, interrupting what possibly was an eternal loop of flabbergasted blinking and gasping.

I thought about my grandfather who wouldn't say pow-wow because it might be insulting and tried to reconcile this with the group he'd apparently founded. Then my brain caught up.

"They can't call it that," I said decisively.

"I agree," Rafael said angrily. "It's really offensive and —"

"Howl's ancestors escaped from the plantations in the south, and Yowl is Native American," I informed him.

"Yeah," Jackson said. "Al thought that the offensiveness of the name might not be entirely clear to them. Howl apparently asked him if his woman would be willing to carry one of his offspring."

Jackson chuckled while I tried to get my stunned brain to grasp that the old, dark-skinned man had somehow thought it was okay to be member of a group called White Supremacy whilst wanting to have a child with a woman of Indian heritage.

Rafael started laughing, and I did too, albeit weakly.

"Al declined," Jackson said when we'd quieted down.

"I'll talk to Gramps," I said with a sigh.

"There's more," Jackson said.

Of course there was.

"Due to their advanced age, they needed a little artificial happiness."

Artificial –

"Like what? Please tell me they're not smoking shit. Dad will have an actual –"

"They're not smoking weed, babe," Jackson interrupted. "Apparently the doc wrote out prescriptions for them."

"Prescriptions."

"For small blue pills."

Rafael started laughing loudly, and I turned to stare at him.

"Know about those, do you?" Jackson asked smugly.

Rafael stopped laughing immediately.

"What?" I asked, and Jack turned to me with a smirk on his face.

"Viagra."

Well, Jesus effing Christ.

Now what?

CHAPTER 20

Erections

If anyone ever thinks about talking to their grandparents about erections, I have a piece of advice; Don't.

It actually started out as a date with Rafael, so the erection part was a surprise. Or, yeah, not really but I hadn't expected that part to be about Grandpa Hunter, who was our chaperone for the evening.

We went to Bubba's because it was the only place Gramps said he'd go to and since Dad was standing on the porch with us, and since he was scowling, Rafael sighed and nodded. A small bar in a small town full of werewolves was clearly not where he preferred to go on a date. I didn't mind because that bar would be full of people I knew, and I was petty enough to want to walk in there with Rafael.

Melissa Moose and her friends, sans the one she

lost at the karaoke-event, sat at a table in the center of the room. The only way to stop myself from shouting out a satisfying but smallminded and highly inappropriate, "Whaddyasaynowbeyatch," was to bite my tongue until I felt the taste of blood.

We moved forward, and one of Melissa's girlfriends squealed loudly when she got a closer look at Rafael. Since she'd been in the middle of gulping down a deep swig of beer, napkin-accompanied mayhem erupted, and Loosey Moosey had to retire to the restrooms to repair her makeup.

"I don't like you," Grandpa Hunter said to Rafael as we sat down in a corner. "But that was hilarious. Might not be a suck-a-duck-evening after all."

"Grandpa," I said warningly. "You promised to behave."

"No."

Since he actually hadn't made any such promise, I had nothing else to say and decided to go and get beer for us instead. Rafael went with me, and we had a minor discussion about paying for our beverages. I lost, and when Rafael had paid the openly laughing barman, who incidentally also was Jackson's second cousin, we had another discussion about who would carry the beers back to the table. This led to a small kerfuffle, and I yanked a beer out of Rafael's hand, somewhat forcefully.

"Ha!" I exclaimed rather loudly, and accidentally slammed the beer into something soft.

Then Loosey Moosey had to turn around and go back to the restrooms and repair her makeup once again, but she really should have known better than to stand that close to me.

"I'm warming to you, cherub," Grandpa muttered when we'd gotten another beer and were back at the table.

Rafael seemed unhappy with this epithet, so I decided to change the topic, and brought up the subject of clubs with offensive names.

"Of course I know what white supremacy is," Gramps said calmly. "We're reclaiming the name."

"From whom?" I asked, dumbfounded.

"From the white supremacists."

Well, duh.

"Why?" Rafael asked, which I thought was a pretty danged relevant question.

"Why not?"

I couldn't come up with one single good reason, and we were busy staring at Grandpa when Grandma Hazel sat down at our table.

"What are we talking about?" she said happily and dipped her tongue in the froth at the top of her Margarita.

"My club," Grandpa said.

Things went downhill from there, and I can't explain exactly how the discussion moved on from a club with an offensive name to the topic of erections. But it did.

"Well, if you're going to procreate, you need one," Grandpa Hunter explained, and I whimpered.

I felt Rafael slowly move his hand under the table, and grab hold of mine. His thumb caressed the palm gently, and a shiver went down my spine.

"I know that," Grandma said patiently. "No one likes a man with a limp –"

"Yieee!" I squealed.

"What?" Gramps asked. "You were conceived. How do you think your father –"

"Yieee!" I squealed again, a lot louder this time.

The owner of the bar was apparently curious because he approached with three fresh beers.

"What are you talking about?" Bubba asked and put the glasses on the table.

"Erect penises," Grandma replied happily.

I let go of Rafael, grabbed hold of a beer and downed it in one go. All of it.

Bubba turned and walked away without another word, but I saw his shoulders shake so either he was crying or laughing. I assumed, not crying.

Rafael was suddenly also laughing, so hard he had to tilt his head back and hold on to the table. Loosey Moosey stared at us. Everyone else stared at us too. Jackson's second cousin was laughing into his phone, which meant Jack was laughing too.

And that was the good part of the evening. After that, it seemed as if everyone in the bar was talking about erections, clubs, or clubs where one had erections. Several men of various ages queried Gramps how one applied for membership in White Supremacy, and there was a disturbing number of women surrounding our table. I spent most of the evening with my eyes closed.

Rafael was still chuckling when he dropped my

two overexcited grandparents and me off, and he was about to kiss me when they had disappeared but ended up laughing into my mouth in a way that wasn't sexy at all.

I huffed and walked inside.

✳✳✳

"I'm joining you on your next date," Elsa said. "Maybe Biff will let me be the chaperone."

"Don't. Won't be nearly as much fun without the old geezers," Joel said, sighed, and added, "We've been to Bubba's almost every night since we moved up to Nowhere, and this goes down when we spend one night at the house watching a goddamned boring movie. Can't believe we missed the whole thing." He grinned and added, "The gossip mill claims it was the best night since someone let a rabbit loose in there."

Oh, goody. I was apparently more entertaining than watching a pack of wolves rip a small fluffy bunny to pieces in a small bar.

I had to walk away from my friends for a while because we were at Tiaso's and I was working. The place was packed, and the tips were absolutely fantastic, but it also meant that I was über-busy. This was unfortunate since Elsa had found a hand-drawn picture of the amulet among a pile of old papers. She'd been asked to return the documents to the wizards but tried to explain to me what it looked like.

"Pentagon," she shouted while I poured shots for

three men who claimed to be wise but mostly looked unusual.

A huge man immediately leaned in closer to Elsa. He had lots of long, unruly, black hair, an equally black beard, more muscles than anyone I'd ever seen – and I had seen plenty – and a tee announcing to the world that he was a happy camper.

"What?" he asked.

"What?" Elsa echoed.

"What what?" the man asked.

"Wh –"

I quickly handed out the shots to the men in front of me, sidestepped back to Elsa, leaned over the counter and growled.

"She started it," the man said with a sweet smile.

I glared at him, which led to nothing at all. Then Elsa poked him in the ribs and murmured, "We don't understand. Please explain."

"You called out my name," he said softly.

The happy camper was apparently called Pentagon, and there were plenty of jokes I could have made, but I didn't. He looked at Elsa as if he wanted to gobble her up in one bite, and I was pretty sure he might be good-looking somewhere under all that hair, so I figured she'd want to gobble a little right back.

She smiled blandly and nodded, but turned back to me, effectively dismissing the man. He shrugged and walked away. A sigh of relief from the bikers pushed my hair back, and I stared at Elsa.

"What the why?" I asked.

We'd known each other a long time, so she deciphered that easily.

"Not interested," she murmured.

"Why not?"

"First of all, he looked like the yeti, which really doesn't do it for me. Secondly, I found out the other day that I can only have kids with another unicorn, and since I'm pretty much the only one... what's the point?"

"Kids?"

I wasn't going to have kids in decades. I'd practice making them, but I had no immediate plans on actually having them.

"I know, I'm just being silly," Elsa said with a grin. "Anyway. The amulet is small, pentagon-shaped, and has a small blue stone in the middle."

"Silver or gold?"

"Probably silver. Looked like it."

"How big?"

"A bit more than an inch across perhaps. Slightly less in height."

Okay. So, we were looking for a silvery blob with a blue stone.

"Hey, babe. Heard you and the douche had fun."

My eyes met Jackson's, and I tried really, really hard to not laugh. I did, though, and told myself it was because I could see the hilarity of our disastrous evening. It had nothing to do with how Jack's blue eyes glittered when he held back his own laughter.

"Hey," Joel said and sat down. "Not going to another bordello in my life."

They had apparently finished getting statements from red-light-ladies working in places paying the disgusting wizard protection fees.

"Hello there, sweetie," Rafael murmured and sat down next to Joel. "Can't wait to go on another date with you. I had such a great time."

Jackson's smile faded away, but Silenus chuckled instead.

Then a short but broad biker leaned forward and hissed in my face, "Why do you get all the hot ones?"

It took me a few seconds to realize that it was a biker of the female variety and wondered if I should share with her that showing cleavage, washing one's hair and applying makeup helped. Or that shaving, anywhere, really, but in particular on one's face, was not a bad thing when one was in the market for a hunk.

She looked brutal, so I settled for, "Beats me."

"Yeah," she sighed, and grunted, "Jaeger."

I could have told her that grunting and drinking Jaeger was not the way to get a hot man. Then I noticed the brass knuckles with small spikes on both her hands and decided to pour the requested shot instead.

"Did you find anything out?" I asked Joel when the bar had calmed down a little.

"All the girls say the same thing," he said. "The wizard protects them. They don't know why or from what, but they all pay him. Jack has statements from them, and I have given him all the information I could find. Bank statements, information about property

GOING NOWHERE

the wizard owns, and so on."

"Huh," I said and frowned. "Does Malachï have any family?"

Joel squirmed and made a face.

"You're not gonna like this."

"What?"

"He bought a new house just a few weeks ago. Huge place, close to Forest Park, right across from St. Johns Bridge."

That was a bit strange. The wizards usually lived in a condo in a skyscraper as close to downtown as they could afford. The only wizard I knew of who lived in a mansion was the Az, and that was because he was married to my mother, and Nim witches always lived close to natu –

"Which one?" I squealed.

"What?" Jackson asked, and both Elsa and Rafael straightened and was watching me apprehensively.

Since I was about to jump over the bar and maul something, I probably had a look on my face that was unflattering.

I did not care.

"Which. One," I hissed, glaring at Joel.

"I don't know. Probably Poppy. Could be Iris."

I raised my hands toward the ceiling and growled so loudly four customers got up and left.

"Kitty, calm down," Jackson said, so I growled at him.

"Kitty," Rafael murmured and tried to take hold of my hand.

"I'm gonna kill her," I growled.

"Who?" Silenus asked, but backed off a few steps when I rounded on him.

"The only reason a wizard would buy a huge place up by the park, that close to St. Johns Bridge, is if he plans to marry someone who will need to live there."

I trailed off, and for the first time in my half-werewolf life, I felt the tingles of fur sprouting underneath my skin.

"Which would be a Nim witch," Joel clarified. "And the only available Nim witches of marriageable age are..."

"My goddamned sisters," I yelled.

The bar was suddenly completely silent, but then Elsa leaned forward.

"Kitty," she said calmly. "Calm down."

"No," I snapped.

"Don't make me fart," she snapped right back.

The bikers standing closest to her took a few steps back, and Silenus' eyes popped wide open.

"You're a unicorn," the huge man called Pentagon suddenly said.

"Yes," Elsa hissed without letting her eyes leave me for a second.

"Huh," the man mumbled.

"What," I snarled and glared at him.

He suddenly grinned crookedly, and his soft brown eyes twinkled.

"I guess I'm gonna impregnate your friend in a not so distant future."

CHAPTER 21

Kitty-cat

When Elsa had stopped hyperventilating, Pentagon informed her that he could wait until she was ready.

"No need to start a family immediately," he said jovially. "We'll wait a few days, and then we decide."

"You should go away," Elsa said hoarsely.

"No," he said pleasantly. "I don't think I should."

During the hyperventilation, it had become clear to us all that he was a super affable guy. Between pressing a big, brown paper bag into the hands of a distraught Elsa and throwing equally distraught bikers across the bar, Pentagon had informed us that he preferred to be called Pen. Or whatever we felt like calling him as long as it wasn't his actual name.

I promptly informed him that my name was Hibiscus but that I preferred to be called Kitty, which made him lean over the bar and kiss my cheek.

Jackson disapproved and slapped Pen in the head, but his hand got stuck in the masses of black hair, so he only got a sweet, happy chuckle in return and then they spent five minutes untangling the mess.

Once Elsa was breathing normally, things calmed down. A couple of the biker brethren disliked how Pen was hovering over Elsa, but he just smiled at them, and their angry words somehow morphed into them buying him beers. Jackson also got Pen a beer, and they sat down to talk for a while, which made Elsa's nostrils flare. I gave her a Jaeger which calmed her down again.

Rafael informed me that he had to leave because his cousin, Jesus, was in jail and needed someone to post bail but that he'd enlisted Joel and Elsa to ensure my safety.

"Jesus... as in...?" I prompted.

"Jesús Hernandez, babe."

Okay, goody. Hernandez was pretty much not Christ, which would have been very very unsettling.

"What did he do to end up in prison?"

"Jaywalked."

His eyes were warm with happiness, and I could tell he wanted to share how in the hell someone could jaywalk badly enough to get himself into a situation where bail needed to be posted, but his phone beeped.

"Gotta go, sweetie," he murmured, moved my hand to his mouth and kissed it gently, and left.

The biker babe who had questioned the fairness of me getting all the hot guys started sobbing.

"That was so romantic," she sniffled.

A tear leaked out of her eye, and she wiped it off with the back of her hand, which was stupid, mostly because of the brass knuckles she wore. One of the spikes tore a long, angry cut across her cheek. I ignored a scowling Jackson and got busy handing out antiseptic wipes, band-aids, and Jaegers.

When Silenus and I had closed the bar, Joel and Elsa waited for me outside. Elsa still seemed stunned, so I pulled the paper bag out of her hands and put it over my head, thinking that a bit of silly goofiness would snap her out of her stupor.

"Wheeeere is Elsa," I drawled, and heard her giggle.

I moved around with my arms stretched out and tried to catch Elsa, or Joel if I was lucky, and we were laughing.

Then they both suddenly went silent.

"Hey," I snapped. "Where are you?"

"Here," a deep voice said ominously.

Without warning, I was unceremoniously pushed into a car, the door slammed shut, and I heard the lock snap. Then we were moving. I was about to remove the stupid bag from my head when I felt the cold metal of something I suspected might be a pistol on my arm and froze.

"That's right. If you move, I'll shoot you."

Oh, God. Oh, my friggin' GOD. He would shoot me.

I really didn't want to be shot.

He'd said not to move but he couldn't see my eyes

under the bag so I glanced down to ascertain if he perhaps was trying to be humorous. It would be mildly amusing if he were poking me with, say, a small twirling baton or possibly a big fountain pen. Or whatever that wasn't a gun. He wasn't bluffing, so I closed my eyes while I tried to figure out what to do and decided pretty much immediately that not moving would probably be in my best interest.

I was about to find the courage to talk to the man when the car stopped, and I heard a familiar crackling sound.

"Don-uhh," I managed to get out, and then everything went black.

I woke up in a small box. My legs were bent, and my cheek was pressed against my knees. My arms had been pulled forward and tied together in front of my shins. When I tried to straighten, the top of whatever I was tucked into blocked any kind of movement.

If it hadn't been for the small gap by my right foot where a small glimmer of light seeped in, I would have shat myself.

"Help?" I whispered.

"Shush," a soft voice murmured.

I opened my eyes widely and tried to move because the voice had come from inside the closed box. Someone else was in there with me.

"Who –"

"Shush," the voice repeated. "Listen."

At first, I heard absolutely nothing, but then steps approached.

"I can't protect you much longer," someone said, and my eyes flew wide open because that was a voice I recognized well.

The Az.

"But –"

Another voice and one I hadn't heard before.

"You have to find the amulet. Why the hell were you stupid enough to steal it?" the Az asked sourly.

"I just borrowed it. Poppy wanted to see it so –"

The Az huffed, and I closed my eyes again. Something that was a little more than a sneaky suspicion had entered my mind. I knew who the other man was.

"Fool," the Az hissed. "I can't believe you dropped it, but you have to find it."

"I'm getting close," the other man murmured.

"Well, get closer." There was a short silence, and then the Az snarled, "Not to me, idiot."

There were a couple of quick steps, and I heard water running from a tap. The sound came from... underneath me?

"Where did you lose it?" the Az asked.

"Not saying," the other man murmured.

"Why?"

I didn't hear the answer because they were walking away, so I counted seconds until I thought five minutes had passed since the sounds disappeared. Then I took a deep breath.

"Hello?" I whispered.

"Hello," someone answered.

"Where are we?" I asked.

"They locked us into a kitchen cabinet."

What? Who the hell did that?

"Who are you?"

"Lucas."

Say again?

"Seriously?"

"Yes," Lucas hissed angrily.

I took a deep breath, and when I did, I realized that;

a) Lucas wasn't a he, and

b) Lucas was not human as much as

c) Lucas was feline.

I twisted my legs apart a little and managed to turn my head by tucking my jaw between my knees. In the gray shades in front of me, there was indeed a small, sleek and completely black creature.

"You're a cat," I said stupidly.

"I know."

"I'm not," I informed Lucas.

"I know this too," Lucas said calmly. "Wolf and witch."

I stared at the yellow eyes who looked back at me with a calm unblinking stare.

"Lucas?" I asked.

"My protector calls me that. He's a fool."

"You look like a miniature panther," I said, and added, "I could call you Lulu instead?"

The cat made a small movement with her head as if she was preening.

"Lulu. I like," she crooned.

"I don't want to be in this cabinet anymore," I said and pressed my elbow to the side as hard as I could.

The doors rattled a little, but they didn't open.

"Push harder," Lulu said calmly.

Well, duh.

I slammed my elbow into the doors repeatedly, but something was blocking them from opening. The only remaining option seemed to be to push with my whole body, which meant I'd fall out when they opened.

That would suck, but everything already hurt so whatever.

I took a deep breath and threw myself against the door. The creaking sound gave me hope, so I braced and prepared to try again.

"Kitty?"

I froze and stared straight ahead.

Was that... Al?

"Open the goddamned cabinet!" I shouted and pushed at the doors with my shoulder.

Then I suddenly fell out of the cabinet and straight into Al's arms.

We stared at each other for a stunned second, but then he crouched to place me on the floor.

"What the —" he cut himself off, looked around and grabbed a knife from a set decorating the wall.

My hands were swiftly cut loose, and I whimpered when blood returned to my arms and legs.

"We should leave," Lulu said. "Now."

Al dropped the knife and stared at her.

"You're talking," he rasped out.

"So are you," she retorted and looked at me. "Leave? Now?"

"Yes," I squealed.

Without further ado, we were running, or in my case mostly limping, following a small black cat toward an entrance which suddenly seemed weirdly familiar. I'd been in this house before.

Al threw the door open, and we burst out on Decateur Street.

"That fucking asshole!" I shouted.

Then we stopped and stared at a rather substantial crowd of people standing on the sidewalk outside the house.

My parents and grandparents were staring back at me. Joel, Elsa, Pen, Jackson, and Rafael were surrounding them, and they also stared at me.

There was a lot of staring going on, one might say.

"Kitty?" Grandma Hazel asked finally as if she'd never seen me before.

"Yes?" I asked back.

"You're hugging a cat," Dad said.

Lulu had indeed jumped into my arms, and I held her small warm body close to my chest. Being half a werewolf, I was supposed to dislike felines intensely, but I didn't.

Her scent soothed me and felt sweet and soft and happy.

"What the hell?" I shrieked. "I was kidnapped. Some a-hole locked me into a goddamned tiny cabinet. If it weren't for my pal, Al, I would have died in there. Who cares if I'm hugging a cat?"

Dad winced and walked toward me, eyeing Lulu carefully.

"We were coming for you, honey," he said. "Jackson and I were tracking and picked up your scent."

"I scryed and came as soon as I'd turned out the fire in the backyard," Grandma said.

"I asked the keychain," Rafael said.

"Got the license plate," Joel murmured. "Hacked into security cameras and found the car."

Big tears started rolling down my cheeks. They had all searched for me and had indeed been there to break me out of Genie Decateur's kitchen cabinet.

"Kitty," Jackson murmured gently.

"Kitty," Rafael murmured gently.

I looked at them and moved toward the man I knew I could rely on whatever happened.

"Dad," I sniffled and walked straight into my father's arms.

He howled and reared back, staring at Lulu.

"She bit me," he snarled.

"Did not," Lulu said. "I yawned, and he walked into my mouth."

✳✳✳

"I was powerwalking," Al said.

We were in my parents' house in Nowhere, I had shared what happened to me. Elsa and Joel had explained how a flash had made them both faint and how I'd been gone when they woke up, and Al was about to tell everyone how he'd saved me.

"Powerwalking," Dad echoed as if the concept was unfamiliar to him, which it probably was.

My dad was not a powerwalking kind of man.

"Yup," Al said. "My woman read an article about Nordic walking and got me a set of poles, but I'm not ancient. I'm also not too hip on looking ridiculous, so I hid them in Cathedral Park. Was on my way to get them when a car stopped next to me. Fat, fugly dude carried someone inside, and I recognized the butt. Waited. Went inside. Let Kitty out, and here we are."

"You recognized my butt?"

"Of course," Al said. "It's –"

The sound Dad made was angry, and it stopped Al from further describing my derriere.

"Biff," Jackson murmured. "You really can't blame the man."

Dad growled at him too, but Jackson growled back.

When this had gone on for a while, I lost interest, so I leaned my head on Joel's shoulder and drifted off toward dreamland. Lulu was on my lap, and she'd been sleeping for a while already.

"Kitty," someone murmured, and I managed to raise my heavy lids. "Did you see who kidnapped you?"

"Saw his sleeve. Stains of beetrooty purple on it. I was at Genie Decateur's house. My guess?" I mumbled and didn't wait for anyone to confirm that they indeed wanted to hear what my guess was.

"Malachï."

"Yes," Lulu hissed suddenly. "He brought you to the house."

"How would you know," Dad asked sourly.

He had apparently still not forgiven Lulu for yawning in a way that made it possible for her to credibly claim she hadn't bit him.

Which she totally had.

"I used to be his familiar."

I looked down on the small animal perched on my lap.

"Used to be?"

"I'm your familiar now," she declared.

"Okay," I said and felt a wash of warmth pass through my core.

Then she started purring.

The silence surrounding me was well beyond stupefied.

"But you're a werewolf," Jackson said, which I knew I was, so I didn't respond.

"You're a little stupid, but you're hot, so I forgive you," Lulu informed him with what looked like a smirk on her cat-face.

"Bet this will be interesting," Rafael said and leaned forward to let his hand glide over Lulu's head.

"You're hot too," she said, tilted her head back and looked at me. "I'm gonna like living with you, my little Kitty-cat."

CHAPTER 22

Procreationist

Dad went with Grandma Hazel to find out what had happened to Genie Decateur and came back purple-mouthed and drunk off his Scandinavian werewolf-ass. I was eating breakfast when they got back so when my mouth dropped open, a piece of bacon fell out of my mouth and onto the table. Through the open window, I heard my father, the werewolf alpha and sheriff in my hometown, sing.

"Kaaalinka, kalinka, kalinka moya!"

My brows went up. Was that... Russian?

"Vashadu yashibashi malinka, malinka moya!"

He tried to move his feet in a dance that was not something I'd seen performed locally and assumed he was also attempting to dance in Russian.

Grandma Hazel was dancing too, but she was laughing so hard she had to double over, and since she kept dancing with her skinny butt in the air, it looked kind of funky. Dad had raised both his hands and was alternating between snapping his fingers and clapping his hands.

Sometimes his hands missed each other, and when he suddenly slapped himself in the head instead, both he and Grandma Hazel cheered loudly.

"Holy crap," Elsa breathed out.

"I agree," Pen said genially. "His accent is godawful."

Elsa's head snapped around, and she speared him with a hard glare. This was the twelfth hard glare she'd speared him with since he showed up on a bicycle early that morning.

"What are you doing here?" she snapped.

"Waiting for you to let me impregnate you," he said with a sweet smile.

Joel started laughing.

Janie tore her eyes from the spectacle outside to stare at Pen.

Then Jackson walked through the back door, closed it quietly and sat down at the table.

"What's going on?" he asked.

"Huh," I rasped out and gestured toward the two fools in the front yard.

Grandma Hazel straightened abruptly and threw her hands out, which made her stumble a little.

"I never knew you were such a great dancer, Biff," she squealed, and declared, "I'll teach you how to pole-dance."

"Yes!" Dad yelled and pumped his hands in the air

as if he'd won an Olympic gold medal. Or the lottery. Or whateverthefudge. "I always wanted to pole-dance!"

Slowly, I leaned forward and rested my forehead on the table.

"Kill me now," I mumbled.

"Why?" Pen asked, sounding utterly confused. "I think he'd be good at it. He's got some serious hip-action going."

I straightened, and we stared in silence at my father and grandmother humping imaginary poles and shaking their shoulders. They were singing, and my brows went up when they shared loudly that they both apparently had been to a motherfucking mountaintop where they had heard motherfuckers talk. Or something.

"Right," Janie said calmly and stood up.

When she had gotten the situation in hand, and the two drunken fools had sobered up, helped by a few select chants from Grandma, we sat on the porch.

"Dad," I murmured.

"Not a word," he growled.

"We won't ever talk about it," Jackson promised solemnly and earned himself a grateful look. He winked at me and added, just as solemnly, "But we'll never forget."

"So," I said loudly before Dad could maul Jackson. "Did you find Genie?"

"Yes," Grandma Hazel said. "We found her in the basement, locked into the laundry room."

"Is she okay?" Elsa asked.

"Sure. She was quite happy, actually. Got all her washing and drying done, which is why we were celebrating."

Yikes. Genie Decateur was apparently made of sterner stuff than me.

"She confirmed that it was Malachï who kidnapped you, Kitty and that he did it because you're investigating his activities," Dad said with a sigh in the general direction of me. "He needed money to fund the kind of life your sister would find acceptable, and he decided to supplement his income with payoffs from the bordellos."

"So, let's go and talk to the Grand Wizard," I said impatiently.

"He's on a retreat somewhere up in the mountains," Dad muttered. "Contemplating the mysteries of the universe. Back tomorrow."

"Okay, then we'll go talk to Blaïse tomorrow. Will you go with me?" I asked.

"I will go and talk to Blaïse. You may come with me," Dad countered.

We stared at each other, and I should have backed down, but I didn't.

"Guess it'll be good if you're there, Biff," Jackson murmured. "You'll have something to talk about, after all."

Every head on the porch turned toward Jack, and he was grinning. Widely.

"Yeah?" Dad grunted suspiciously, indicating that Jack's grin was just a little too cocky.

Which it was.

"Sure," Jackson said casually. "You've both been to a motherfuckin' mountaintop, so —"

I hadn't known it was possible to run that fast whilst laughing hysterically.

Or run almost that fast whilst roaring angrily for that matter.

***

Since Silenus had told me to not show up for work on account of what he labeled, "my ordeal," Janie asked me to do her shopping.

Or, yeah. It wasn't her asking me as much as it was her ordering me.

"Grocery store and pharmacy," she said, handed me two lists and her credit card.

It felt like being fifteen again, and I was about to tell her I'd pay when I remembered my condo payment. It was due in less than a week, and I'd counted my cash.

If tips kept coming and I found the damned lovebird, I'd make it.

If I bought groceries, I wouldn't.

Fifteen again it was.

Since I was in no hurry, I chatted with the guy who worked in the pharmacy while he punched the stuff from Janie's list into the register. Pat was a wolf, had been in my class in high school and had had an enormous crush on Elsa. He still had one if the number of questions he asked me about her was any indication. I steered the conversation into the break-in they'd had, mostly because I wasn't sure what would happen with Elsa and the perpetually good-humored Pentagon.

"It was the weirdest thing," Pat said. "Nothing was stolen."

"Really?" I asked.

"It looked like things were moved around. Almost like when we've done a stock take."

"Someone had been here to count your inventory?" I asked, thinking that yes, indeed.

That was weird.

"Only —"

Patrick stopped speaking and blushed a little.

"Only what?"

"Products for men," he muttered and bagged my items speedily.

Oh, shit.

I had a fairly good idea what products for men he was talking about.

Viagra.

Which meant I knew who had broken in to check the stock.

Grandpa Hunter, Howl and Yowl.

Well, shit. I had to get that situation sorted out before they got themselves arrested.

Karma was on my side because an immediate solution presented itself in the form of Becky from the community center ambling innocently along the sidewalk as I exited the grocery store. I waved her down and started chatting about the weather. When that topic was exhausted, which was two sentences later, I figured I'd been polite enough and that there was nothing to do but to lay it all out.

"Do you want to procreate with my grandfather?" I asked.

Becky walked into a lamp post and didn't step back from it.

"Nuuh," she said.

I watched the pretty woman standing there with her nose pressed to the steel and wondered if gramps' genetic superiority would outweigh her stupidity, or if any kids they might have would perhaps be half-witted.

"He says you do," I informed her, which made her back away from the lamp post and glare at me.

"No," she snapped.

"Says you want his genes," I elaborated.

She stared at me for a long time and then she closed her eyes.

"The old fool should get a hearing apparatus," she muttered.

"What?" I asked, not following her train of thought.

Her eyes snapped open, and she glared at me in a way that made me take a step away from her.

"I asked him to give me his jeans," she snarled. "As in; his pants," she added, and I took another step backward, just in case. "Because it was," she inhaled deeply and bellowed, "LAUNDRY DAY."

Okay. Alright. Jeez. Calm the hell down.

This was what I thought but didn't dare to say

because her eyes were suddenly yellow which meant she was close to shifting.

And I really didn't want to get mauled.

"Okay," I said soothingly.

"I told him I wanted his jeans and if he didn't want to give them to me, he should give them to Maria or any of the girls," Becky snarled.

Okay, well that explained why he thought there were scores of women ready to procreate with him.

"I'll talk to Gramps," I said quickly. "Simple misunderstanding."

"Why would I want to hump that old goat?"

I had no answer to that question and consequently said nothing at all.

"Talk to him," she snapped and walked away.

I waited until she was far enough away to not hear me, and snarled back at her, "I already told you I would."

Then I went home, put the groceries away, and walked up the stairs to Grandpa Hunter's borrowed studio above the garage.

"Hey, Kitty," he said with a happy smile.

I sat down and sighed.

"I have shit to tell you," murmured.

It had occurred to me that he might be upset about the fact that he wasn't going to be quite as sexually active as he'd anticipated.

"Okidoki," he said, sat down and watched me with eyes that were just as happy as his smile.

There wasn't anything else to do.

I had to tell him.

"I talked to Becky and you misunderstood because she never wanted your genes but instead she wanted your jeans as in your pants because she was going to wash them for you, so the procreation part is out of the question and you have taken all that Viagra for nothing."

Then I inhaled, which I needed, and leaned back.

He blinked a few times and then he grinned.

"It wasn't for nothing," he said calmly. "I enjoyed having a boner."

"Yuh?" I managed to say, and immediately wished I hadn't made it sound quite as much like a question.

"It's been a while," Grandpa Hunter elaborated happily. "It also made getting my willy into the crotch enlarger a lot easier."

Oh, God.

This was the exact moment I would die, I was sure of it.

Since I didn't and since Grandpa didn't say anything, I sucked in air and changed the topic.

"What will you do about the club? Dissolve it?"

"Absolutely not," Gramps protested. "We can't do that now when so many of the local boys have applied for membership. Howl is teaching them the signal tomorrow."

I blinked, but he grinned as he raised a hand, stuck his thumb in his left ear and wiggled his fingers.

"We're thumbing our ears at the stupid white supremacists," he explained.

"The expression is to thumb your nose."

"We're unique," he retorted.

They were that.

"But —"

Gramps interrupted me, which was good because I wasn't sure what to say.

"We'll just change the statutes. I'll reword it. Take out the part about being procreationists. I'll replace it with a paragraph about being shuffleboard players."

Okay. That was a pretty harmless activity.

"What will you do with the rest of the, um... pills?" I asked.

"Maybe Jackson wants them?"

I was pretty sure Jack didn't need them.

"No," I said, and hoped he wouldn't ask me for details.

He didn't.

"I have my share in a nice little matching pill box, so I'll just hold on to them until I find someone who needs them."

"You do that," I said.

"Perhaps Biff would want a few."

Biff?

As in; my dad?

Eek!

CHAPTER 23
Hibiscus de Chamontelette-Brown

I woke up before the alarm which was a massive surprise, mostly since it probably was the first time that had happened. I lay there in stunned amazement and wondered if I was becoming an actual adult.

Then I heard the rattle of small pebbles on my window and grinned.

Nope. Not a grownup. And neither was my grandmother, it seemed.

Grandma Hazel and I went to see Genie and have breakfast. Or, since I refused to partake of anything at Ms. Decateur's home, it was the other way around, and we stopped for pancakes before entering a house where I'd been held captive just a few days before.

"I'm so sorry," Genie said, and squeezed my hand

in a way that likely was supposed to be reassuring, but mostly hurt.

"You didn't kidnap me," I murmured and pulled my hand away from her death grip. "It wasn't your fault."

"I designed the kitchen."

I blinked.

"Could have asked them to install bigger cabinets, and I would have..."

"Don't worry about it," I said, but she just kept talking.

"... if I'd known someone with your booty would be locked into one of them."

Huh. Slightly insulting but not entirely incorrect.

"Okay," I said, lacking anything more eloquent to add. "Will you go with us to see the Grand Wizard?"

"If we go before ten o'clock. I have an appointment at eleven that I can't miss."

"What are you doing?" Grandma Hazel asked. "If you need me to come with you, I'd be happy to –"

"Yes, please," Genie said immediately. "I'm nervous."

Her night in the laundry room had apparently not been as easy on her as she'd told my dad.

"I'll be there for you," Grandma said and patted Genie's hand.

"Thank you, Hazel. You can help me place it."

Place what?

"Place what?" Grandma echoed my thoughts.

"The strawberry."

Huh?

"Str –"

"I'm thinking left."

"Left what?" I asked, and I really shouldn't have.

"Butt cheek."

I closed my eyes.

"I'm getting a tattoo," Genie clarified. "It's my first, and I wanted a beetroot, but Josito can only do strawberries and skulls." She smiled happily and added, "I didn't want a skull."

Hoo-kay. Next topic.

Crap. There was no topic available in my mind because my brain had stuck on the visual of a not fully clothed Genie Decateur, old as dirt and skinny-saggy everywhere.

With a strawberry tattooed on her left butt cheek.

"How exciting," Grandma Hazel squealed. "I could do a skull."

No. No, no, no. Yikes. Jesus. Whatever.

"Let's go and see the Grand Wizard right away," I blurted out.

"Not a good idea," my backpack said.

I turned slowly and glared at it.

"Lulu?" I asked.

"What?" she snapped. "I wasn't going to stay in a house with millions of werewolves. And I have to protect you."

"From what?" I asked exasperatedly.

"Yourself."

Cute but completely unnecessary.

"We are leaving, and we are leaving right now," I declared haughtily. "I'm calling everyone from the car to see if they want to join us."

***

Dad didn't pick up. Joel did, and he brought Elsa, and since Elsa was there, Pen ambled up to us while we waited for Jackson and Rafael.

"Shit," I muttered when I saw Grandpa Hunter next to Jackson in the Nowhere PD vehicle he was driving. Then I saw Rafael's sleek, black Porsche where Silenus somehow had squeezed himself in, and added, "Double-shit."

"Kitty, perhaps we should wait," Jackson said.

"Or perhaps we should go now," I retorted calmly, hoisted Lulu up on my shoulder and walked toward the entrance of what Grandma had assured me were the wizard's headquarters.

They wouldn't let us enter.

I glared at the pale, thin individual who had been a man less than two weeks and hence was an incredibly junior wizard. He swallowed, which made his Adam's apple bob unattractively, and I gathered up all my abilities. My witch blended with my wolf and to my surprise, I felt taller and somehow... regal.

"Tell Grand Wizard Blaïse that Hibiscus de Chamontelette-Brown requests an immediate audience to discuss topics of utmost importance to him," I said with so much haughty power in my voice the young man shrunk back and picked up his phone without further ado. "Jeez," I muttered. "He could have just let us in."

"Pretty impressive, Kitty," Joel murmured in my ear. "Pretty damned impressive."

Before I could grin at him, the doors swung open, and we marched inside.

I kept my abilities flowing, and since I was surrounded by a group of others with various skills, the air crackled with power as we walked across a courtyard and into a big room. At the other end of the room stood a tall man, flanked by four men in wizard's clothes. Lulu hissed softly, jumped off my shoulder and disappeared.

I kept walking until I was a few steps away from the men.

They stared in silence at me.

I figured this was normal within wizard-circles, so I stared back at them. Their long shirts and wide pants looked rather silly but also comfortable. I decided to sneak one of the Az' sets into my bag next time I visited Mom. He had a blue one that was pretty, and it would look great with my hair. Or else I'd get the green one which matched my eyes.

The tall man suddenly coughed.

"Blaïse," I murmured and tilted my head in a way I'd seen royals do in costume dramas on the TV.

"Hibiscus de Chamontelette-Brown," he drawled.

"That is my name," I informed him and chastised myself silently because, duh. That had been a pretty stupid thing to say, so I added, "As you know."

"Where are you from?" the man asked.

"Nowhere."

He raised a brow, and I raised one of mine.

"Are you sassing me, young lady?" he asked coolly.

"I sass you not," I replied and raised my other brow, which felt less regal and more idiotically surprised, so I lowered it quickly again.

"Hm," Blaïse retorted.

"I have news best suited for your ears only," I declared magnanimously. "It concerns one of your..." I made a brief pause and tried frantically to recall the hierarchies among the wizards. "Underlings," I finished the sentence and wondered if that even was an actual word.

Perhaps I should have said minions instead? Or nothing at all?

"One of my underlings," Blaïse said slowly.

"Hm," I said, which was what he'd murmured earlier so I figured it would be an okay thing to say.

"Walk with me Hibiscus de Chamontelette-Brown," he said and made an impressively authoritative sweep of his hand. "I know your mother."

"Fuchsia," I murmured as if he didn't know.

I hoped he didn't know she was currently Fucksia.

He stumbled slightly, but then we walked away from the others. He took me into a covered hallway which I could have sworn I'd seen in one of the Lord of the Rings movies, and I explained what we'd learned about Malachï.

"I'm surprised," he said when I was done.

"I can imagine. It was a considerable surprise to my friends and me too," I said, thinking that; wow.

I totally sounded like a grownup.

"Do you have proof?"

"Unequivocally," I murmured, and wondered if I should tell him about Joel's findings, me being kidnapped and the statements Jackson had collected.

I also hoped I got the meaning of the word right. The Az had used it, so it seemed like something a wizard would enjoy hearing.

"What would you expect from me?"

What? Was the man stupid, or something?

"He should stop extorting the businesses," I stated. "Let go of Genie Decateur," I added and smirked. "Stripping Malachï of his powers for the next century would be a very nice bonus."

"He is engaged to your sister," Blaïse said.

"Half-sister," I corrected him. "I'm sure my parents and sisters would agree that such a man is not... fitting into our family."

I was actually not that sure, but it had sounded good, and I totally did not want that douche showing up at Christmas dinners and the likes. Eating Thanksgiving turkey whilst watching a bobbing sweep of orange hair would totally destroy my appetite.

"And in exchange, you will not bring this to the High Grand Wizard?" Blaïse prompted.

Huh? There was a High Grand Wizard? Like an über-wizard?

"I will not bring it further, but I will not lie in case I'm questioned," I countered.

He stopped and looked at me.

I looked back at him.

He was quite handsome if one liked longhaired, older men with goatees.

It had never been my thing, but pre-Pen, Elsa would have been all over this man.

He grinned suddenly, and yeah. Elsa would have been salivating. I swallowed and wondered if I might not be on the verge of drooling just a little myself, actually.

"We have a deal," he said, gray eyes soft with humor. Then he waved his hand imperiously, and added, "It's done."

I faint scream echoed in the distance, and my brows went up.

"Holy Mo —" I didn't think holy moly was noble enough, so I amended my statement to "Mother," and added for clarification, "Of Nature."

There, I thought. Mothers and nature. That was what Nim witches were all about, wasn't it? The skin around Blaïse's eyes crinkled slightly, and then he led me back to where the others were waiting.

"It has been a quite surprising pleasure, Miss de Chamontelette-Brown," Blaïse said and indicated that the doors to the courtyard should be opened which I assumed meant the audience was over.

"The pleasure was all mine, Mr..."

I had no clue what the darned man was called, but he didn't seem to mind.

"Under the circumstances, I think you should call me Blay," he said.

Uh, what?

No, this I should not do. Mostly because I would not be able to do it with a straight face.

"I'm Kitty," I murmured.

Then I tilted my head in that regal nod again and walked away.

The others followed, and no one said a word until we were standing on the sidewalk outside the brown double doors again. I quickly explained what we'd talked about, what Blaïse had agreed to and they stared at me.

"You do know he's a mind reader, right?" Grandma Hazel wheezed out.

A mind –

Well shit.

A faint echo of laughter echoed from inside the house, and I turned to look back through the doors. Were they laughing at me? Probably, I decided, and couldn't blame them. I would have laughed at me too.

In the courtyard, a small, turquoise shape suddenly swept through the air, and I blinked a few times, wondering if it indeed was what I thought it was.

A lovebird.

"I need peanuts," I exclaimed. "Don't close the door," I ordered the guard-wizard-man-boy and he froze. "Does anyone have any peanuts?" I whispered frantically. "Or olives. Chips. Snacks. Now. Now. Now

_"

"I have these," Grandpa said and put a few in my hand.

"Thanks," I murmured and walked back into the courtyard.

Then I stretched my hand out and started whistling Oh Susanna. A door opened and Blaïse, again flanked by several men, was watching me from it. I ignored them and kept up the snappy tune. I only knew the first line but didn't let that deter me and repeated it insistently.

When the bird turned midair and aimed for me, I knew that it was indeed the missing Peanut. The lovebird was turquoise as his owner had specified and had the black face she'd described. I saw this clearly when he landed on my hand and started nibbling on the small blue pills I was holding out toward him.

This meant that I was unfortunately also holding the pills out toward the Grand Wizard of Portland and what possibly was the entire universe.

Oh, God. My goddamned grandfather had given me –

I tried to close my hand, but Peanut had apparently liked the taste, so he started pecking my fingers with a surprisingly sharp beak.

"Ow," I squealed. "Stupid goddamned animal," I snarled and stepped back, swiping at the bird to get him to stop attacking me.

Then it occurred to me that this was not an exemplary Nim-witch behavior, and my eyes turned to the group of wizards. Before I could figure out what to say, a black streak flew through the air.

"Let's get out of here," Lulu murmured, and she did this around Peanut who was held firmly in her mouth.

That seemed like an excellent idea, under the circumstances, so I turned toward the stunned wizards.

"I wish you a thoroughly enjoyable day," I declared and tried to walk out of their headquarters in a dignified manner befitting the place.

But I mostly ran.

Well, shit, that had not gone exactly as planned, although unless Lulu was hungry, I'd managed to capture Peanut.

Lulu waited with the others, and this time, I didn't stop the young man from closing the doors.

"Don't eat him," I snapped at my familiar and gently pulled the bird out of her mouth.

"I'm a vegetarian," Lulu murmured.

I almost dropped the bird but managed to tuck him into my backpack and pull the zipper. He flapped around a bit but seemed to settle down almost immediately.

"Really?" I asked.

"Totally," she said. "Except for mice. I eat mice. I actually don't eat much else because I love mice."

"So, you're really a micetarian?"

"Yes!"

"Okay."

CHAPTER 24

Believe you me

I was going on another date.

I'd lost track of whose turn it was, but after a flurry of messages back and forth, Rafael informed me that it was Jackson's turn. They had also decided that since Rafael had taken me to Bubba's, then Jackson would too. Rafael might join us later.

I stared at my phone and wondered what would happen if I simply didn't show up.

Would Jackson and Rafael go on a date without me?

Then I had lunch with my father who couldn't seem to stop laughing.

I thought he'd be upset that I had gone to see Blaïse without him, but the Grand Wizard had called Dad approximatively four seconds after the double doors were shut and had laughed so hard he dropped his phone.

Twice.

And I was apparently invited back for another audience whenever I felt like going.

Mom had called Dad too, and she had been less amused, a circumstance Dad shared with a rather unattractive relish.

My sisters had all left messages on my phone. Poppy was inconsolable, but the others were covertly gleeful in a way I thought was about as attractive as the sneer on my father's face. I sent a group message to them saying that hooker-extortionists were not my favorite people, which got me a dozen replies that I ignored.

When Dad had gotten himself under control, he leaned back and sighed.

"Only you, Kitty."

"We got what we wanted, didn't we?" I asked.

"We sure did," Dad said calmly, but his mouth twitched as he added, "I sass you not? Salivating? Really?"

Goddamned mindreading wizards.

To change the topic, I quickly informed Dad about my date with Jackson.

Dad promptly retorted that he knew about it, my grandparents were unavailable, and Pentagon would be the chaperone.

The enormous, hairy unicorn had apparently overheard Dad and Jackson and offered to be of service. I tried to convince Dad that either of my grandparents would be infinitely preferable to a yeti-looking man my own age, but my efforts were in vain.

Grandma Hazel was apparently spending time with Genie, which I assumed meant Grandma had gotten herself a tattoo.

Grandpa Hunter had a club meeting

After some high-pitched questions from me, I discovered that Pen and Dad had bonded over their admiration of Elsa. This had been further enhanced by Pen declaring that he wanted to get married, was on the market for a house, and preferably one that needed some work because he was a carpenter and also a plumber who liked to put up tiles.

Elsa had been there to hear Pen's announcement and shared that she did not want to marry him, something Dad told me with a chuckle was merely a minor, "Lover's spat."

I informed him that they weren't lovers, and if they were to spit, then Elsa still held the record from Saint Honoria of the Immaculate Transformation High School. By two and a half yards to the runner-up.

That shut him up and we finished lunch in a highly satisfying silence.

Then I returned Peanut to his grateful, tearful and according to her, also blissful owner. I collected the reward and went to Tiaso's for a completely uneventful shift, but the unexciting evening made me a little bit nervous.

It felt like the calm before the storm.

I wasn't wrong.

The second Jackson and I walked into Bubba's, a

shitstorm did indeed erupt, starting with Melissa Moose who descended upon us, crying hysterically and doing it on Jack's shoulder whilst trying to lick his left earlobe. It took both Bubba and Parker to pry her strong arms off Jackson, and then he had to lean on the bar to catch his breath.

Loosey Moosey wrapped herself around Parker instead, and the look on his face would have been hilarious if he'd been able to actually breathe.

Then Pentagon stepped in and murmured something which made Melissa faint, and we were free to walk over and claim a table in a corner.

"I don't want her," Jackson muttered and indicated Melissa with his hand.

She was being hauled up from the floor by three of her girlfriends and Bubba, and I got an unwanted crotch shot.

Loosey Moosey apparently wore really huge, beige granny-panties.

"Believe you me, I would not have been on a single date with you if I'd for a second thought you still wanted that," I said decisively, and meant both Melissa and her unattractive undergarments.

Jackson's face softened which sent a shiver down my spine, and the sounds from the bar seemed to fade away until it was just him and me in a bubble of happy.

"Believe you me?" he murmured and used a hand to move a few strands of hair away from my cheek in a soft caress. "You've been watching movies with your grandmother again?"

"Yes," I whispered even though I hadn't.

His eyes started laughing, and he leaned forward until I could feel his lips on my ear, which incidentally sent another shiver down my spine.

"Maybe we should –"

"Hello, my pretty-kitty," a voice murmured in my other ear.

I twitched and unfortunately did this in a way that slammed my head into Jackson's mouth. He grunted and reached for the stack of tissues Joel wisely had placed on our table as we sat down.

It would have been helpful of me to assist him in wiping off the blood from his lip, but I was busy staring at a skinny-muscular, black-haired woman who was smirking straight in my face.

Belinda, my lesbian vampire friend, had left her lair and joined the crowd at Bubba's.

"What are you doing here?" I squeaked.

"Aren't you happy to see me?" she asked in a voice full of syrupy-sweet fake concern. "I thought you loved lesbians?"

"I love lesbians," Pen cut in with a smile. "And they love me!"

Uh, what?

"Pentagon!" Belinda said in what was disturbingly close to a squeal.

"Sugarpuff!" Pen said in what also was disturbingly close to a squeal.

They hugged as if they hadn't seen each other since the second world war, which might actually be true considering the life spans of both vampires and unicorns.

Elsa put her beer down with considerable force. I stared at the openmouthed group around the table. Jackson started laughing and had to wipe off more blood from his split lip.

Since there were no empty chairs, Belinda sat down on Pen's lap.

"I can help you with that," she said and nodded toward Jack's mouth.

"No thanks," I said.

"Aha. I thought the angel looked sexually frustrated," Belinda said. "Now I know why."

"What are you doing here?" I repeated rather forcefully.

"I want to thank you, of course," she replied as if my question was borderline stupid, which it was not. "Pimpleton is gone, profits are up. We're grateful."

"You're welcome," I said. "What he did wasn't right, and Blaïse got that immediately."

A curious Bubba put a pitcher of free beer on the table, got himself introduced to Belinda, my lesbian vampire friend, who informed him that she wanted to be called Bellie. He left laughing. Again.

We talked for a while about Malachï, and how he'd not only helped himself to some of the profits but also to some of the girls.

Ewe.

"He carried an amulet around with him," I said quietly, and Bellie leaned forward which made her top slide upward and her pants downward.

"Thong," someone whispered reverently behind

Pen, which made him glance down and grin happily.

"Indeed, it is," he confirmed. "Black lace." Elsa made a strangled sound, and he looked at her in confusion. "But you wouldn't look good in that." When Elsa made another rasping sound, he added, "Mauve. Sage. Or... perhaps a pale blue would suit you better. I'll see what I can find."

I decided to ignore the fact that one of my best pals looked a little bit like a guppy and turned back to my vampire friend.

"Did you see the amulet?" I asked Bellie.

"Amul – Oh, you mean his shiny little container. Yes, he was showing it off almost as often as his private parts."

Ewe, again. My sister had been lucky to get out of that entanglement.

"He's dropped it, and we don't know where. Can you look around at Pussy-Pussy-Pussy and see if it's lying around there somewhere?" I asked.

Bellie promised to ask Mellie who was in charge of the cleaning crew, and I was about to thank her when a loud voice from the door boomed.

"She should be here somewhere!"

Well, shit.

A very familiar troll walked in, accompanied by four other trolls. They were thankfully not naked, but they were many, and they did not look happy. Trolls actually never seemed happy, not even when they laughed, but still.

I moved slowly to place myself behind a couple of ferns hanging from the ceiling in huge pots.

"Get them out of here," I wheezed to no one in particular.

Jackson leaned forward, and his shoulders started shaking in a way I assumed meant he was laughing. Then he straightened and, yes indeed. He was laughing.

Loudly.

The group of trolls turned and caught sight of Jack, and the others around the table.

And me.

When Mellie's brother started toward me, I ran, but so did he.

And so did his friends.

I rounded the bar with five trolls at my tail. Everyone in Bubba's had moved to the sides except Loosey Moosey, so one of the trolls ran into her, and they both went down. I did another lap around the bar with four trolls chasing me.

"Stop them!" I yelled, and Bubba stepped forward.

He caught another with his chest and then I kept running with three trolls at my tail. I also had to jump over Bubba every time I passed him.

"Kitty!" my troll-nemesis roared.

Oh, God. He knew my name. He might even know where I lived. He might —

I ran faster, but since a few of the trolls were in a not so good shape and had a hard time running with their big bellies, I caught up with them and consequently had to slow down.

The front door suddenly opened, Rafael walked

in, caught sight of me running around the bar completely surrounded by trolls and started laughing.

I scowled at him and forgot to jump over Bubba. As I went down, one of the trolls had had enough and stopped abruptly, so I barreled straight into him.

He was sweaty.

Troll sweat is slippery.

So, I slid off him, and my speed propelled me straight into the wall.

"Kitty!" Mellie's brother bellowed, and I tore down a framed picture and held it out in front of me as a shield.

He moved to the side.

I moved to protect myself from whatever he felt like doing.

He moved again.

This went on for a while, and I wondered why no one helped me instead of laughing; what could have gone wrong with my love song counseling session; and what the hell my grandfather, Howl and Yowl were doing in the image I held out in front of me.

Then I decided to try to reason with the distraught man-troll in front of me and stopped moving.

The troll didn't, and his arm came toward me with alarming speed. His small fist hit me in the head, and as I went down, I heard him scream hysterically.

"Omigod, no, no no! I only wanted to thank her!"

CHAPTER 25

Plain sight

Janie was a fantastic step-mom. Beyond fantastic, actually.

And she was above her usual awesomeness when one of her cubs were injured.

Which I was.

It wasn't life-threatening, and it would fade in a few days, but I had a shiner the size of Montana from Melvin-the-troll's fist.

He was crying all over me when I came to, flat on the floor of Bubba's, still clutching the photo of Grandpa Hunter and his cronies to my chest. Then I was picked up and placed on Rafael's lap. Jackson pressed ice to my eye and wiped off goop. Neither of them men were laughing. Pen was also uncharacteristically unhappy and threw trolls around in a whirlwind of troll-mucus which didn't stop until

Elsa stepped in and got him to calm down.

"I'm so sorry," Melvin sobbed. "I only wanted to thank you. Mellie told me what you did for my woman and me, and we are blissful." He sniffled and added, slightly louder, "Wonderful."

"Okay," I murmured.

"JOYFUL," Melvin suddenly roared and started crying again. "And I clocked you."

It sounded mostly to me as if he was full of nothing but shit, but I decided to not share this and asked for a Jaeger, which I got. It tasted just as awful as it smelled, but it perked me up.

When the trolls had calmed down and withdrawn to a dark corner of Bubba's, we had a surprisingly fun evening. It was slightly disturbing that both Rafael and Jackson treated me as if we were on a date, but then Loosey Moosey got rolled up paper napkins pressed up her nostrils to stem a rather persistent blood flow from hitting the floor with a troll on her back, and they made her look perfectly ridiculous.

That perked me up too.

Elsa and Pen had a heated discussion in a corner which ended with Pentagon laughing, shaking his head in apparent disbelief, and kissing Elsa's knuckles.

Joel hooked up with one of Melissa's friends and disappeared early, grinning wickedly.

Parker disappeared with another of the Moosey-girlfriends, grinning the same way.

Then Rafael kissed my cheek and murmured that he'd see me at Tiaso's the next day, and Jackson took me home.

I didn't get any kisses on the porch because Janie waited for us. Someone had called her, apparently, and she went into über-stepmom-mode immediately. Jackson was unceremoniously shoved toward his car, and I was led inside to eat large quantities of cookie-dough and lie down with an ice-pack on my face. For some reason, my troll-misfortune relieved me from chores for the next seven days, and since I hoped to be back in my apartment within that timeframe, it meant that I'd done the last dishes in a long, long time.

Eating cereal straight from the box might be pathetic, but it meant a lot fewer dirty plates.

I fell asleep with the pack of ice still over my eye, and a steady trickle of cold water over my cheek and neck woke me up the next morning.

When I'd showered, dressed and felt ready to face the day, Janie gave me a latte and told me to sit on the porch for a while. I sighed sadly, hoping this would put her in a pancake-making mood, and walked outside to watch Lulu run around in circles.

The spot where Grandma Hazel had scryed to find the whereabouts of the amulet was apparently a good place to chase mice. Grandma had seen something old and something small in her visions, and I wondered if it simply had been the mice running around her bowl.

Leaning on the wall, I thought about the evening before and had to chuckle a little at the stupidity of using a framed photograph to protect myself from a troll.

What the hell had the old geezers been doing in the picture anyway? They had done the stupid ear-thumbing at the white supremacists, and held their other hands out toward the camera, showing off some –

Then it hit me.

Malachï had borrowed the amulet but had dropped it somewhere, which could very well be at Pussy-Pussy-Pussy.

Bellie had called it a container, which really was a box of some sort.

Grandpa Hunter had told me he kept his pills in a matching pill-box.

Elsa had described the Azdjakzian amulet as a small silvery blob with a blue stone on the top.

Grandpa had been to Pussy-Pussy-Pussy a while back to ensure things were twitching and shaking, and he could have found it.

And the blue stone would match Grandpa Hunter's small blue –

"Gramps!" I yelled.

Then I ran.

***

"I can't believe Hunter had it all this time," Grandma Hazel said and shook her head.

I was behind the bar at Tiaso's again, the shiner had changed from a swollen and angry, red mess to a greenish shade around my eye, and Silenus laughed every time he looked at me.

"Gramps was quite surprised when I came running up the stairs," I muttered.

The elderly woman next to him in his bed had been equally surprised, and her squeak matched mine.

After some confusion and loud explanations on my part, Grandpa joined me on the floor, rummaging through the old-wolf-clothes which were spread out all over. These garments included a mustard colored thong I accidentally touched, which made me squeal even louder than before.

Then Grandpa Hunter pulled a small pill box out of the pants he'd located.

It was made of silver.

Pentagon-shaped.

And had a blue stone on top.

He gave it to me, and I felt the power from it immediately.

It was indeed the Azdjakzian amulet.

"What did the wizards say when you returned it?" Jackson asked.

I grinned.

"Kitty," Rafael said quietly. "You did return it, right?"

I grinned some more and tried to wiggle my brows but scowled, on account of shiner-induced pain.

Silenus started laughing, Grandma Hazel smirked, Jackson growled, and the front door opened with a loud crash.

My mother and stepfather marched through a bar

that was suddenly quiet.

"Mom," I said and did my regal nod.

Then I ignored the pain and raised one brow.

"Oh, stop it," Mom snapped.

"Welcome to this humble abode," I said calmly and moved my hand in what I thought was a fair imitation of Blaïse's authoritative gesture. "What can I get you?"

"Don't be ridiculous, Hibiscus. Give it to me," the Az snapped. "You have no knowledge about the power it wields, and —"

"I would be happy to give you the item you commissioned me to search for," I drawled. "Except, there's this teeny-tiny matter of the fee."

The silent bar went even more silent, and while watching the two furious individuals in front of me, I wondered what the word for that would be.

Silenter? Silencious?

"Fee?" Mom asked.

"Uh-huh," I confirmed and nodded for extra emphasis.

"Don't be ridiculous," the Az snapped. "Hand it over."

"Are you saying that the word of an Azdjakzian can't be trusted?" Wee-the-weasel suddenly murmured.

I waited silently.

"I never —"

"Hello everyone," Al called out. "Beer and a Jaeger, babe." Then the tense atmosphere hit him, and his brows went up. "What?"

I grinned at him, poured a beer and reached for a shot-glass.

"This wizard here…" I filled the glass with Jaeger. "My stepfather," I drawled, and pushed the glass toward Al. "He promised me a million bucks in reward for the Azdjakzian amulet. I have the Azdjakzian amulet in my possession, and we are just discussing the transfer of funds."

"I never promised you a million," the Az protested sourly.

"But you did?" Al said, the picture of innocent surprise. "I was here when you did. You wore ugly shoes and a green ladies-tee. Kitty asked specifically if the reward was one million, and you replied," He paused, frowned, and added, "Unequivocally."

"Yu-hup," Silenus said with flair. "I was here too. Three independent witnesses."

The Az opened and closed his mouth a few times.

Then my father walked into the bar.

"Okay," Mom snarled immediately. "We'll transfer the reward."

"And when you have done that, I will transfer the amulet," I said affably.

Dad choked on nothing at all but thankfully kept quiet.

"Do you expect us to do it now?" the Az said haughtily.

"I can do it for you," Joel offered.

The looks he got from my mother and stepfather were scorching, but he just grinned. The Az' nod was barely visible, but Joel kept smiling as he put his index finger on his phone.

"Done," he said to me.

I hadn't for the life of me thought they'd actually give me that amount of cash and had been perfectly prepared to negotiate. A thousand would have been fantastic, as far as I saw it, but I wasn't going to share that and kept my cool.

Then I put a hand in my pocket, pulled out the amulet and placed it on the counter, but kept my hand over it.

"One question," I said. "Is it silver?"

"White gold," Mom snapped.

Aha. That explained why Grandpa had been able to handle it. We might have figured it all out a lot sooner if someone had just told me. Or not.

I pushed the small thing over the bar. The Az snatched it up immediately, and let his fingers slide over it.

"What the —" He cut himself off, unscrewed the lid and stared into the small container. "What is this?" he asked dumbfounded.

"Grandpa Hunter says you can keep them," I shared with a smirk. "Don't take more than one each day, or you will have problems."

Dad choked on the beer Silenus had placed in front of him.

Joel barked out laughter.

The Az closed the box again and placed it in a purse he had hanging across his chest. The turquoise thing was decorated with small pink beads, and I wondered if he'd borrowed also this item from one of my sisters.

"I'm leaving," he announced and walked away.

Mom stared thoughtfully at me for a while, and I let her.

"I think we might have underestimated you, Hibiscus," she murmured. "Blaïse was very impressed."

"Tell Blay I said hey if you see him," I said casually and pretended that I had to pour a couple of Jaegers.

"It isn't proper to address the Grand Wizard with a nickname."

"He asked me to," I retorted, and wondered if it wouldn't be totally appropriate to throw a beer in her condescending face.

"Fuchsia," Dad rumbled quietly. "You should leave."

To my surprise, she did, although it could have been because the Az was holding the door open and was waving his hand in a way that looked silly.

"Thanks," I said to Dad, but turned my head and extended my gratitude to Joel, Al, Wee, Silenus and pretty much everyone else. "Who wants a free shot!?" I squealed.

"Kitty," Dad muttered. "For Christ's sake. Don't spend your whole reward on drinks."

I told him the size of my reward.

Then we had shots, and when Dad had picked his jaw up from the bar and gotten an ice pack from Silenus, he had one too.

"Only you, Kitty," he muttered. "Guess you'll move out again."

"That guess would be accurate," I confirmed. "I'll go talk to my landlord tomorrow afternoon."

"We'll miss you," he muttered and wiggled his glass to indicate that he wanted another shot.

"Pretty sure it'll be great," Rafael said with a smirk.

"Yup," Jackson confirmed.

While my father roared angrily, I poured Jaegers and laughed.

"Kitty," Elsa said quietly. "Let's talk tomorrow morning before you sort out your place."

"Sure," I said. "Why?"

"I have an idea."

"Oh," Grandma Hazel squealed. "Can I come? I love ideas!"

CHAPTER 26

Lost? Go Nowhere

Everyone apparently loved ideas, if the crowd on my parents' front porch was any indication. Elsa told them to leave, and after some pushing and shoving, they did.

Then it was just Elsa, Joel and me, and that's when Elsa blew my mind away.

"I hate my job," she began the mind-blowing, and went on, "You only work a few hours every week, Joel, and you're bored out of your mind."

Their eyes met, and after a beat, Joel sighed and nodded.

"God, yes, I am," he said. "Have thought about getting a hobby but I can't find one I like."

"You don't even have a job," Elsa said and looked at me.

I was about to protest because selling drinks

might not be the most amusing occupation on the face of the planet, but it was a bona fide employment. She ignored my imminent protests with a sweet smile.

"We're good at finding things."

We were.

"We should start a private investigator business."

I stared at her and Joel started laughing.

"That'd be something," he murmured, but I could hear in his voice that he was intrigued.

"You got all that money from the Az," Elsa said to me. "We could add what Joel and I get if we sell our condos, and it'll be enough to buy a building downtown.

I blinked.

"No, it isn't. Do you even know what a building in Portland would —"

"Not downtown Portland, Kitty. Downtown Nowhere."

What the... what?

"Yeah," Joel drawled. "It would be more than enough. There would be money left to keep us going for quite a while even without clients."

"There's a building up for sale," Elsa went on. "Next to Bubba's. Three stories. Business on the ground floor. Two apartments on the second floor and they've converted the attic into a big loft."

"Shit. You're right," Joel said.

My mind was whirling with ideas suddenly. The three of us living in the same house. Running a PI-business. Going to Bubba's. Finding shit for a living.

Having fun.

"You'd move up here permanently?" I asked.

"Totally," Elsa said. "I love it here. I would prefer to have a place of my own and not mooch on your parents, but the town is great. The people are even greater."

"Joel?" I asked.

"What she said. Plus, my condo downtown is the size of a stamp, and it's quiet up here. For someone like me... You know I like when it's quiet. The buzz from all the systems running in a big city isn't my thing."

Okay.

Right.

Shit.

Could I move back to Nowhere permanently?

"What would we call the company?" Joel asked, as if it was a done deal already and, oh my God.

It was.

"Nowhere PI," I said. "We'd have the best slogan ever."

"What?"

I grinned at them and raised my hands in a shrug. "Lost? Go Nowhere."

✳✳✳

Dad cried when I told him and Janie about our plans. He said it was because he got dust in his eyes, but it wasn't. His only daughter was moving back to Nowhere and had together with her friends bought a house which would need repairs and maintenance and fixing up until the end of time.

So, he cried a little.

"Who placed bets on Jackson versus Rafael?" I asked to distract everyone.

My father still got comments about the beetroot-induced dance performance, and he didn't need to get teased for crying a few adorable tears of joy. At least, not by anyone other than me.

"Come on," I coaxed when no one admitted they'd been part of a bet that was stupid. "Just tell me."

Everyone slowly raised their hands.

Everyone.

Even Rafael and Jackson, which was just plain ridiculous.

"Huh," I grunted mostly because I didn't know what to say.

Then a phone rang, and Joel, Elsa and I stared at it.

It was our newly acquired business phone.

"Good afternoon," Elsa answered chirpily. "You've called Nowhere."

This caused a minor confusion, which the three of us probably enjoyed a little too much, and then we had our first client.

"Another dog?" Joel murmured, and I could tell that he wanted to get into the systems to start searching.

"A Poohuahua," Elsa said with a nod. "Ran off two weeks ago and has been spotted down in Salem, drinking tequila."

Yikes.

"I see Mexican food in our future," Joel said with a content sigh.

"And mariachi bands," I added happily. "I'll go down there tomorrow and get the lay of the land."

Fun times; you may commence, I thought with a grin.

"It'll be great to have you living up here," Jackson suddenly said, looking pleased with himself, with me, and the situation in general. "Bubba's tonight?"

"Or dinner downtown?" Rafael cut in, apparently equally pleased. "There's this small seafood place, just by the river..."

Both suggestions sounded nice, but I had made my mind up and didn't hesitate to convey my decision.

"I don't want to date you, Rafael. You're too good-looking," I said.

Jackson smirked, but I turned to him.

"And so are you," I shared. "I won't date you either."

Jack's smirk faded quickly, and I watched the two smoking hot but thoroughly confused men in front of me.

Then I raised my chin, straightened my shoulders, and told them.

"I've decided that I'm gonna pass on both of you and find me a regular dude. Someone like Al."

"An older guy?"

"Al, but my age," I elaborated.

They looked at each other in surprise and started laughing loudly.

I growled which made them turn and laugh right in my face.

"I will," I insisted.

They kept grinning, which looked ridiculously good on both of them.

"Yeah, we'll see about that, Kitty," Jackson said calmly.

"Indeed, we will," Rafael added with a smirk.

Well, shit.

Dear reader

This book is a project I started on Wattpad, mostly to do something different, and differently – I have enjoyed myself thoroughly, and I hope you did too as you entered the crazy world Kitty lives in!

If you are eager to read more about Kitty and the others, please let me know by adding a review where you picked the book up, on Goodreads (www.goodreads.com), or let me know via my web-site and social media (@lenanorthbooks).

/Lena

ABOUT THE AUTHOR

Lena North is an author and illustrator who likes to read more than anything. Curbing her desire to curl up in a corner with a book are a couple of big, crazy dogs, two fantastic daughters who aren't crazy at all - and a head full of stories. Lena writes fantasy, adventure, romantic and happy stuff mixed up with sorrow and hardship, and since life is way too short to go around feeling grumpy, there has to be a bit of laughter here and there...

For more information, go to:
www.lenanorth.com

Or connect with Lena on social media
@lenanorthbooks

www.ingramcontent.com/pod-product-compliance
Lightning Source LLC
Chambersburg PA
CBHW050015180626
46810CB00002B/422